GIRLS

Pushkin Children's

GIRLS

Written and Illustrated by

ANNET SCHAAP

Translated by Laura Watkinson

Pushkin Press
Somerset House, Strand
London WC2R 1LA

Copyright text and illustrations © Annet Schaap 2021
English translation © Laura Watkinson 2023

Girls was first published as *de Meisjes* by Em. Querido's
Uitgeverij, Amsterdam, 2021

First published by Pushkin Press in 2023

The publisher gratefully acknowledges the support
of the Dutch Foundation for Literature

N ederlands
letterenfonds
dutch foundation
for literature

1 3 5 7 9 8 6 4 2

ISBN 13: 978-1-78269-378-9

Designed and typeset by Tetragon, London
Printed and bound in the United Kingdom by Clays Ltd, Elcograf S.p.A.

www.pushkinpress.com

For my other sisters: Fredrike, Jenny,
Anne Mirjam, Trudy, Dette, Janneke,
Peet, Inge, Judith and Lynn; Annemieke,
Ivette, Cécile and Mirjam B.

If you are a monster, stand up. (…)
If you have been broken, abandoned, alone
If you have been starving, a creature of bone
If you live in a tower, a dungeon, a throne
If you weep for wanting, to be held, to be known,
Come stand by me.

— CATHERYNNE M. VALENTE

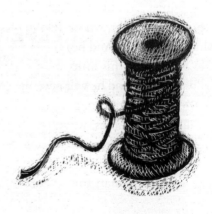

MR STILTSKIN

Gold

The girl sits spinning in the sunshine in the back room. It's mid-afternoon, the light is soft, and all is well. The potatoes have been peeled, the soup has been on for hours, and her mother has been lying in her grave so long that it feels normal and almost isn't sad any more. Her father is whistling in the flour room.

The wind carries the scent of cut grass in the sunshine, of warm straw.

A prince is on his way here, she thinks, as she often does. A prince from afar, who is coming to fetch me. His horse as white as his teeth. And he will let me sit behind him. We will ride at a gallop, his arms warm, his hair long, as gold and yellow as straw, and he will never let go of me, the man I love.

Men rarely ride along the path by the miller's house. Just her father sometimes, when he has to make a delivery. The mill is a long way from everything else.

But a girl can always dream, and this afternoon her dream feels more real than the summer's day. Everything smells so much of love and straw that she can almost hear the horse's hooves. She gently puckers her lips for the moment when she will need them. After all, a girl had better be prepared.

The afternoon is so soft that she can easily reach her hands through it to what lies beyond, and before she knows it, she is spinning her thoughts into a golden thread. Her dream always has a part two: The Proposal; and also a part three: Engaged! When she has enough time, she can spin it out even further: The Royal Wedding, The Honeymoon, and then Happily Ever After… The thread becomes longer and longer. It gleams in the sunlight.

Just before The Wedding Night, it is time to put on the potatoes. She winds the thread onto a reel and gets up to light the stove.

'Did you make that? Really?'

The miller looks at his daughter as if seeing her for the first time. Her? That dreamy, dozy daughter of his? Who always forgets everything, who never has anything interesting to say… She suddenly made this?

'You spun it? But how?'

She mumbles something vague. He seldom gets a clear story with a beginning, a middle and an end from her.

He rubs one fat finger over the thread. It's good stuff.

What beautiful work, he could say. Or: This is amazing. Well done! But he's not that kind of father. He prefers to point out what she does wrong and where she needs to improve. He doesn't want her to get too big for her boots.

'You could have cooked the potatoes for longer,' he says, munching two at once.

'Yes, Father,' she nods. And she goes on eating, like a good daughter who doesn't get any fancy ideas in her head.

He puts the reel of thread in his pocket.

He forgets it for a while and doesn't think about it again until he makes his weekly delivery to the royal palace.

A tall senior footman peers at the sacks, with a frown on his face.

Oh yes, thinks the miller. There was a worm in the flour last time. A tiny little worm. One worm in an entire sack – big deal! You wouldn't even taste it, as he knows from experience. But who's going to have to pay, as always? That's right: him.

'One more chance, I said,' the red-jacketed beanpole warns him. 'Or we'll find another mill. You haven't forgotten that, have you?'

Of course he hasn't forgotten. But he hasn't had time to mill any more flour this week, so this week's flour is more or less the same as last week's flour. Which he could have sieved, of course. Which he should have thought to do, of course. But there you go.

The footman takes out a little gold sieve with tiny holes. Those worms won't be any smaller now, not after eating flour for a whole week.

Think of something! the miller urges himself, sweating. Use your brain! Come up with a plan! Trying to look more confident than he feels, he slips his hands into his pockets.

Where his fingers find the reel.

'Oh, by the way, um… Peter…' he begins slowly.

'Pierre,' says the footman, correcting him.

'While we're talking, Pierre… I've, um, got something… um, something that might…'

The tall footman acts as if the miller has not spoken and continues to pick at the rope on the sack.

'Something… um… quite extraordinary, an… um…' The miller can feel his armpits growing sticky under his shirt. 'An outstanding op… opportunity. I've got…'

He might as well not be saying anything. The footman is already holding the sieve over the mass of worms that the sack has most likely become. One-two-three and he'll be in there. And four-five-six the miller will be out of a job.

'Gold!' the miller blurts. 'I've got some gold for you!'

The hand with the sieve pauses.

'Gold?'

'Yes! Yes!' The miller almost nods his head off. 'Real gold. Lots of it!'

'And I'm supposed to believe you?'

'Yes! Here! I can prove it! Look!' Shaking, he pulls out the reel. What is he actually giving him? The other day, it really did seem like gold. But actual gold? It can't possibly be. She can't just spin gold out of nowhere, can she, that daughter of his? No one can do that.

Suspiciously, the footman looks at the thread. Pulls a little from the reel. Gives it a sniff.

'And there's more,' the miller says quickly. 'For you. For your boss. As much as you want!'

'Have you found a goldmine on that barren little piece of land of yours?' The footman sneers his sneeriest sneer, but his hand returns the sieve to his inside pocket.

'It's not *a* mine. But it's mine, um, my… err…'

'What are you babbling about, man?'

'My child. My daughter. She made this.'

'Your daughter?'

14

'My wonderful dearest darling daughter.' The miller sighs. He suddenly loves her so much.

For the twentieth time, the king looks at the little reel in his hand. He narrows his eyes.

Could it be? he thinks. Could it really be gold? It would be such a help if it were.

You can't keep plucking a kingdom's feathers forever. And the beautiful peacock that his country once was is now as bald as a frog. Taxes, regulations, fines for almost everything – what else is a ruler to do?

That's right: borrow, and he has done exactly that – and far more than was wise. His creditors are slowly running out of patience.

And depriving himself of any of the things he cares so much about, his clothes, his dainty appetisers, his side dishes, the furnishing of his palace – in short, his entire lifestyle – that would be going much too far. Wouldn't it? He has truly earned it all by… By being the ruler that he is. And that ruler happens to have grown accustomed to his wardrobe, his dinners with many courses, and especially what all of it says about him: how well he has done in life.

So, he does not intend to miss out on any opportunities to replenish the treasury, no matter how small and unlikely they might be. For the twenty-first time, he looks at the reel of thread that his footman has brought to him. And nods.

'The horses, Sire?'

'The horses, Pierre.'

Straw

It is a very different afternoon. It already seems like autumn. It is drizzling and the clouds are low.

The girl is sitting in the same chair, but the dreaming is not working out so well today. Her father's acting strangely, and she doesn't know why. He keeps coming in all the time, looking at her and then going to sit on the bench outside. When she gets up and walks to the back door, he hurries over to her.

'Where are you going?'

'Nowhere.' Where is there to go?

'You just stay put,' her father says. 'Don't go anywhere.'

'But the chickens need to be fed.'

'The chickens can wait for a while. Stay inside. Do some spinning or something.'

'I've run out of wool,' she says. 'I ran out ages ago.'

'So, what did you use last time, last week, to spin that, um… thread?'

'Oh, just something. A bit of straw.'

'Straw, I see,' her father says with a nod and looks out of the window yet again.

The girl doesn't want to be difficult, but she wasn't expecting it to be like this.

Just for a little while, everything had seemed exactly right. She was a bit surprised when all those men came into the small room, with their cloaks and fur collars, and all the soldiers with their helmets and long lances – but then again, not all that surprised.

After all, she had known this would happen one day.

She had always imagined it would be outside, and that for some reason he would be disguised as a simple man, a shepherd boy or something, but that she would recognise him by his beautiful blue eyes, his noble features and his authority as he spoke to the sheep. And that they would immediately fall in love even before he revealed that he was the king.

Would you accompany me to my palace? he would say, and the look in his eyes would be so sweet – how could she refuse?

But when he came into the room, she could tell at once that this man was the king – by his ermine and his crown. Not so much by the rest of him, though. He was already going a little bald, and his teeth were not quite as white as they should be.

He held out his hand, as she had always imagined he would, but not to take hers or to give her a ring. More as if he wanted something himself.

More gold thread? No, she didn't have any.

'But she can make some more. Just like that!' her father called through from the kitchen. There was no space for him in the room.

'Is that right, girl?' Finally, the king looked straight at her. His eyes were exactly right. The bright blue of a lake. 'Did you make this?'

'Spun it,' she croaked; her voice was not cooperating.

'Good,' said the king. 'Bring her to the palace.' He took a handkerchief from his sleeve and hid his face in it. Overcome by emotion, she hoped. But his face looked more as if he thought the place was rather smelly.

'So, do we have a deal?' her father called from the kitchen.

'Shut it, miller,' snapped the senior footman. 'Seeing is believing.'

'And then paying, of course,' she heard her father say. She didn't get time to say goodbye.

The king's horse was white, at least. But she had to ride behind one of the soldiers. The other one took her spinning wheel. Her head did try very hard to glue everything together to make it all beautiful and romantic. But she couldn't quite manage it.

The girl looks around the big dark cellar and sighs. What had she been imagining, though? That she would have her own room with a beautiful view? That she would share the king's bed? She really didn't need much, to be honest. A small room at the back of the palace, where she would be allowed to stay until the engagement was announced – she really hadn't been counting on more than that.

But this…

The cellar is damp with a low ceiling and vaults extending into the darkness in every direction, so far that she can't see their furthest reaches. But she can hear them, because when the footman locks the door the grinding sound echoes from pillar to pillar, and on and on and on into the distance.

Trembling, she strokes the spinning wheel. At least that's something from home, and it comforts her a little.

She had been shocked when she realised what was expected of her.

'Spin more g… gold? Now? Here? I can't do that.'

The king held up the small reel of thread in front of her face, looking at her, his eyes as blue as two lakes.

'You made this, didn't you?'

She nodded.

'Well, then you can do it again, can't you?'

She shrugged.

'I was able to do it then, yes. There, that afternoon.'

'What's the difference? It's your own spinning wheel. And straw is straw. Or was it special straw?'

She shook her head.

'Good. Do your best. I'll see you tomorrow morning.'

'But…' She took her eyes from the spinning wheel and the two big bales of straw and looked up at the king, who had already half turned away. 'Why…'

Then she suddenly understood. He was putting her to the test, of course, to see if her love was true. She nodded.

'You can count on me, Sire,' she said firmly. But he had already left.

We're still only in part one, of course: The Meeting. And this is part 1a: The Test. Part two, The Proposal – that won't happen until tomorrow. If I do all of this, if I have shown my worth. Tomorrow morning.

Is it morning already? The cellar seems just as dark, but hours must have passed by now. She tried, she really did. Her fingers are ruined from trying.

But the straw is still straw.

All around her, there are crumpled tufts of straw, sticky balls of straw and a few pieces of straw-like string with blood on. But no smooth, thin and silky-soft thread.

Let alone gold.

When her hands won't stop bleeding, she can't hold in her tears any more either.

How on earth did she do it that afternoon? She can't remember. The sun was shining, she was humming a tune, and the spinning came naturally. She wasn't paying attention, her hands just did it. Just like that.

'Please, hands! Do it again!'

She shakes her hands until the fingers splash drops of blood, then she wipes her nose, and now there's blood and snot and straw everywhere.

How is she supposed to face the king like this? When she thinks about that, she can't keep her crying quiet any more.

'I can't do it,' she sobs. 'I really can't do it. I can't do anything! Nothing at all!'

The echo bounces her words from pillar to pillar and on into the dark cellar.

Nothing, it says. *You can't do anything, nothing at all.*

Then little footsteps in the distance join in with the echo, as soft as a mouse's pattering. They grow a little louder as they get closer.

Someone is coming.

'Oh oh oh, what's all this? Tears? Tears in the night?'

Out of the darkness steps a little man. His white hair is neatly combed. He is wearing a grey striped suit with a red tie.

'Girls crying? That's not something I like to see.'

I'm not crying, she wants to say, but of course she is. She gives her face a rub, which only makes it dirtier and wetter.

The little man comes and stands right beside her, his head no higher than her shoulder, his beady eyes looking her up and down.

'Ooh, you look a mess. Blow your nose, powder your face, straighten your dress. What have you got to be sniffling about?'

He takes a small lace handkerchief from his inside pocket and places it on her knee. She blows into it. It's far too small to cope with everything that's coming out of her nose. Quickly, she crumples it into a ball. She hopes he doesn't want it back.

'Now, what seems to be the matter? What on earth does a nice girl like you have to cry about?'

With the wet handkerchief, she points at the two big bales.

'It… It's not g… gold,' she hiccups.

'No, I can see that. It's straw. So what?'

'I have to spin it into g… gold…'

'Gold? Gold out of straw?' The little man giggles. 'What a peculiar idea!'

'But I made a promise!'

'Who to? The king? To George?'

She nods. 'He wants me to do it.'

'Ah, that George,' says the little man. 'He always wants something. He wants so many things.'

'But I can't do it!' the girl cries again. 'I could do it before, but I can't do it now-ow-ow!'

George… she thinks, somewhere in a small corner inside her head. So, he's called George. What a nice name.

'Right, so you can't do it. Then why don't you just go and do something else?'

The little man walks around her, touching everything. The straw, the spinning wheel, her knee, for a moment. Then he reaches into his other inside pocket and takes out a small white card.

'May I introduce myself? Stiltskin is the name. Reginald Philibert Stiltskin. Businessman, entrepreneur, benefactor… Artist, in fact. And tonight: Saviour of Girls in Need. So, dry your tears, girl. I'm here to help you.'

'Help me?' Her tears turn the card into a blotchy little white rectangle. 'Can you do that?'

'Oh child, it's not that difficult, you know. You simply reach your hands through reality to what lies beyond, let your wheel do its work and ta-da: gold.'

He takes off his jacket and looks around for a hook. There are none.

'Really?' She gives a shaky sigh. If he could do that, then…

He nods and hands her the jacket.

'Like this, over your arm, don't get it dirty. I'm happy to help.'

'Can you really do it?'

'Few things are simpler.'

He gives the idle wheel a quick spin.

'Oh…' the girl says wearily. 'I was afraid that—'

'But not for free, of course. One good turn deserves another. Everything has a price.'

The relief she felt for a moment instantly evaporates.

'W… What do you want? I don't have anything.'

'Oh, I'm sure you do.' Those beady little eyes look her up and down and up again. 'Everyone has something.'

Oh no, the girl thinks. There is no way I'm going to kiss him. I won't do that. But he's already pointing his finger.

'That,' he says.

She places her hand on the spot he is pointing to, between her throat and her heart.

'No, not that. I can't. It belonged to my mother. I promised I would never take it off.'

'How very loyal of you,' says the little man, nodding approvingly. 'But fine. Then it stops here. I'll just wish you all the best for the future. My jacket, please. Did I give you my card? Ah, yes. Good night, then.'

His voice echoes between the pillars as his footsteps click away. *Good night-ight-ight…*

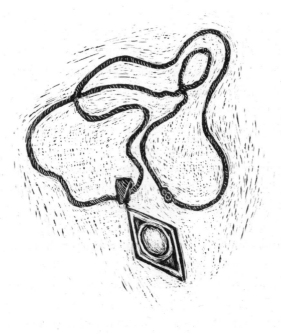

'Wait!' she calls. She reaches behind her neck and starts to unfasten the clasp.

He suddenly reappears beside her and climbs onto the stool. She feels his fingernails graze against her skin, and the necklace slips off.

Bye, Mum, she thinks.

Ring

The key grinds in the lock of the cellar door, and the morning light falls in through the crack. The girl quickly tidies herself up. Beside the spinning wheel are two piles of softly gleaming golden thread. She was so overwhelmed with relief that she barely looked to see how the little man did it. And whatever he did, he did it very quickly, before disappearing with her tiny inheritance in his inside pocket.

She has a vague ache in her stomach because she didn't spin the gold herself, of course, and wasn't that what the king wanted? He must never find out, she thinks. He. George. Oh, George…

And how happy George looks as he runs his hands through the piles of gold thread.

'She's done it,' he says quietly. 'She's actually gone and done it!'

He looks so fresh and handsome, while she is an absolute mess. But still he walks over to her, places one finger under her chin and tilts her head up.

Here it comes, she thinks. It's time for part two: The Proposal. He looks at her with his deep-blue eyes, and she can no longer feel the pain in her hands.

'So, it seems you really can do it, after all,' he says quietly. 'I didn't actually think you could. Good job.'

'Oh,' she says, blushing. What does it matter that his teeth are not white and that his hairline is receding? She is so happy.

The king clears his throat.

'There was something I wanted to ask you. Will you…'

She is already nodding. Because of course she will.

'Oh, really?' he says happily.

'Of course…' George, she adds in her mind. But she doesn't dare to say his name yet. All in good time.

'Wonderful! Then I'll have five bales delivered tonight, or six. How does that sound? You can manage that, can't you?'

'Huh?' she says. 'What?'

'You can't?'

'You want me to do another night?'

'Yes!' he says with a nod.

'No!' She shakes her head.

'No? But just now you said yes. Try to be a little more consistent, girl.'

'B… but I thought…'

'What did you think?'

'I thought that…' She falls silent. Whatever was she thinking? 'I really can't do it again!'

'Ah,' says the king. 'But what if I really, really want you to? You'll do it for me, won't you, darling?'

Darling. That helps. He takes her hand and gives it a squeeze.

'Ow,' she says, because the rings he is wearing are hard, and her fingers are still sore. But they feel less sore when he kisses them one by one. And even less sore when she sees his sweet smile up close. When she nods, the smile becomes even sweeter.

'Alright, then,' she says. 'I promise, Your Majesty.'

'Oh, call me George,' says George. He twists off one of his rings and slides it onto her finger. It has a big stone. So, it is part two, after all, she thinks happily.

But he has already let go of her hand. And he's looking at the gold.

The second night seems to be even darker. And to last even longer. Her neatly bandaged hands start bleeding again – and again she feels desperate. If only she knew how he did it, the little man, but she can't remember. And she does not know how to call him either. And she is not sure that she wants to. She can still feel his little fingers touching her neck. She shakes her head.

'I'll do it myself. Tonight, I'm going to do it myself.' She grits her teeth.

But what can a girl do? With shivering, broken hands and six huge bales of straw that are sitting there silently waiting? Not a lot. Certainly not spin gold. Not a thread, not a shred.

But she is not going to call for him. She will *not* do that.

'Yoohoo? Who was that? Did someone call?' The footsteps come tip-tapping out of the darkness.

Nobody, she wants to say. But she doesn't say it. Her hands lie bleeding in her lap.

'Good evening once again,' the little man says. 'Same girl, same story, I see?'

She smiles, trying to be polite. And feeling rather relieved at the thought that she might be able to stop, that he might take over her task. One more time. Six more bales. For George.

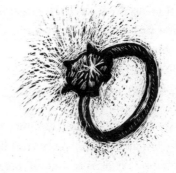

'Well, I'm here now. Shove up a bit. Here's my jacket. And what do you have to pay me with this time?'

She quickly hides the hand with the ring behind her back.

'Yes, that! I can see it, you know!' He takes her hand and holds it up to his face. 'Oh, that's niiice. Twenty carats? Yes, George knows how to win hearts. Go on, then. You might as well take it off already.'

'But…'

'Or not. Up to you.'

She has no other choice.

'How very careless,' George says in the morning. 'Losing my engagement ring so soon? Is that how much my love is worth to you?' She hasn't told him how she lost the ring, or about the little man, or about the exchange. George looked so happy when he saw the new gold that she couldn't bring herself to disappoint him.

'And I was imagining such a beautiful wedding party. White horses, white coach, a big buffet for a thousand guests…'

'Really?'

'Of course. Which is obviously going to cost a pretty penny. I would have liked to say you've done enough now, but I'm afraid I can't. Not yet. It would make me so very happy to marry you, you know. But you understand: only if you—'

'No,' she says.

'Just one more time.'

'That's out of the question.'

'Do it for me, sweetheart. For us, in fact. For our happiness. Here, it's all in your hands. You do want to get married and live happily ever after and all that, don't you?'

Yes, she does. But she really, really, really does not want to spend another night in the darkness with that little man.

Twenty bales, and then that's enough for ever. George has sworn on his mother's grave. And surely she trusts her own fiancé, doesn't she?

Of course, she nodded. But when she looked in his eyes, she didn't know if it would ever be enough.

He has given her a new ring. Fortunately, it's much less beautiful, so it's not nearly as bad if she loses that one too, she thinks. But the little man just laughs at her when she tries to give it to him, that night among the vaults.

'This won't do the trick, girl. I don't want any cheap and nasty fakes, thank you very much.'

'But then what can I…?'

'Oh, I'll come up with something. I'll have a think about it while I'm spinning, hmm? And I'll let you know soon enough.'

He has already sat down. She already has his jacket over her arm.

'But then…'

'You'll have to say yes? Yep, you've got it in one.'

His hair stays neatly in place, and not even a crease appears in his shirt as his hands smoothly transform bale after bale. His little foot on the pedal makes the spinning wheel turn, so fast so fast.

'Let me see. I want, I want… Now, what do I want?…' he hums. 'Hmm, maybe this? Or no… perhaps that? Mmm, that… or this?… What shall I choose? What kind of gift?'

Shivering, she watches him. What price will she have to pay? Her beautiful wedding, her veil, the diamond tiara that George has promised her?

'Yes!' crows the little man when he's halfway done. 'I know. Of course. I choose… your child.'

'My what?'

'Your baby. Your firstborn.'

She laughs in surprise. 'But I don't have any children.'

'I know. And maybe you won't have any in the future. That's not my call. But if one comes along… then it's mine.'

Oh, not to worry, thinks the girl. That's still so far off. If it ever happens, one day… She can't really picture it, as her dreams always end with a sort of vague happily ever after to follow the beautiful wedding. And it's such a relief that it can still go ahead!

If that child ever comes along, she thinks, I'll simply have to make sure not to love it too much. It still seems so distant. And so easy to do.

The night whooshes by, as do the wonderful days and weeks that follow.

Child

Well? Is she happy now?

Yes, she is, but not for long. Before she knows it, she's pregnant. Before she knows it, she's round and fat.

George can hardly wait for his son and heir to the throne.

'Although… children are pretty expensive, you know,' he says. 'Maybe you should give the spinning wheel downstairs the occasional whirl, darling?'

'You said it would be enough, didn't you?' she asks. 'For ever?'

'I did, I did. But why not give it a little go every day?' mumbles George. 'Just in case. You never know.'

Her secret grows along with the child inside her. It colours everything, more than she had thought, outweighing her happiness.

Her father keeps coming to visit the palace at every opportunity. He is delighted and proud. Everyone is so delighted and so proud. But she does not smile. She does not tell anyone why.

'Don't even try to understand,' the king's father-in-law tells him. 'There's no accounting for women and their whims.'

The child is born – and it's a girl.

That's a bit of a disappointment, but George soon gets over it. After all, there's always the next time. The king, who never does anything himself and cannot imagine that anyone else might want to, immediately employs a nanny. Her name is Eline.

'Then you can concentrate on other things, sweetheart,' he says. 'Down in the cellar maybe? Give it another shot?'

She says yes, but she doesn't do it. She just sits upstairs all day, looking at her child, at her eyes, her little nose, the soft golden curls.

This is all I need, she thinks. This is all I need.

Because the not-loving-it-too-much hasn't really worked out. She wants to be with the little girl all the time, to hold her all the time.

She doesn't tell anyone about her secret. But every day she feels it coming closer. Even though she hopes it won't, hopes that perhaps it didn't really happen. Or that she'll pluck up courage to tell George. And that he will stand up

for her and say: 'My child? Taken away by a creep like that? Never.' And he will have the little man banished, beheaded or sliced in two.

She should really say something. Every day, she means to bring it up.

But she doesn't.

She sits by the cradle and keeps looking at her child and then the door. And then back at her child.

The little girl can already lift her head, tries to grab things, smiles at her mother, who doesn't dare to smile back…

And then the door opens.

'Why so startled?' the little man asks. 'You knew I would come. And I keep my word, girl.' He reaches out his little hands. He has brought a pink carrycot with him. 'Go on, then. Give it here.'

'Never!' she says. 'I will never do that.' She grabs the child from the cradle and hugs it tightly to her. 'Eline, call the guards! Someone is trying to kidnap the crown princess!'

'Kidnap?' the little man hisses. 'It's all agreed, fair and square. Stay where you are, Eline.'

'You can't have her! You will never have my child!'

'Don't get yourself so upset. Anyone would think I want to eat her.'

'Eat her?' She clutches the little girl even more tightly.

'Of course not. I'm not a barbarian,' says the little man. 'I just want… a little bit of company, for a lonely old man. That's all, truly. I'll shall give it an excellent upbringing. I've already enrolled it at a very prestigious school… You really have no cause to object, girl.'

She keeps shaking her head.

'Please, no. Please, no…' She starts crying. So does the child. And Eline, who doesn't really understand what's going on, can't help but join in.

'Oh dear,' the little man says. 'I didn't know you'd get so emotional about it. Come on, pull yourself together.'

'Please, don't take her, please… Mr… um…'

The little man freezes.

'What? You do remember my name, don't you, girl?'

'Um…'

'I distinctly remember giving you my business card. You did read it, didn't you?' His eyes spit cold sparks at her. 'I can't believe you don't remember. And after everything I've done for you.'

She searches her muddled head but can't find his name anywhere. The little man takes a few steps towards the nursery door. Then turns around.

'I'll make a deal with you, girl. I'll give you until five o'clock tomorrow afternoon. Then I'm coming for the little one. Unless… you can muster the courtesy to remember my name. My complete name. Then you can keep it. That's a very generous offer, I'd say.'

The door slams behind him.

'Who was that?' asks a shocked Eline.

'I wish I knew…' she whispers into her daughter's curls.

'My daughter? You've promised my daughter to someone else? Whatever were you thinking?'

She is standing in the throne room with the child in her arms, George is on his throne, it's already getting on for five o'clock. All day long, together with Eline, she has done her utmost to dig the little man's name up out of her memory.

And when that didn't work, she tried to find her old dress. His business card must still be in the pocket. They've turned all the cupboards in the castle inside out and upside down. But no dress.

And now she has confessed everything.

'I am terribly angry with you,' says the king. 'And also very disappointed. So, you didn't spin that gold by yourself at all. If I'd known that, then…' He looks at her but doesn't say what he would have done. 'But come, come, I shall naturally have the man in question beheaded. Don't you worry, poppet. Anyone who messes with my child is messing with me.'

She takes a breath and rocks the girl. Hush hush, she thinks. Your father will save you.

'Stealing a child…' The king shakes his head. 'What sort of person would come up with such a despicable plan and…'

'Hello, George.'

The door opens and the little man casts a long shadow right across the throne room.

'Oh,' says the king feebly. 'It's you.' He gulps.

The little man practically skips across the marble to the throne. He gives the girl a wink.

'Your husband and I are old friends. Didn't I mention that? No? And neither did George? He owes me a sizeable sum, too. And I was just thinking this afternoon that I wouldn't mind having it back.'

She sees her husband slump a little on his throne. He looks at her anxiously.

'I don't have it any more,' he whispers. 'Don't you have a little something, darling, um… down in the cellar?'

'You see, girl? I have my finger in plenty of pies. Let's drink to that. And smoke a nice cigar. And then you can let me know, children. Either I get my money back or I get to hear my name. And I don't want it to come from you, George, or it doesn't count. Which will it be? Otherwise, of course, I'll be going home with a sweet little daughter. You tell me.'

Pierre the senior footman is already hurrying in with a tray full of little glasses and ashtrays.

After he's had a drink, the king gets a little more colour in his cheeks.

'Fancy forgetting something like that,' he says crossly to her. 'It just goes to show that girls don't have the brains for important things.'

And they drink to that.

Luckily, the door opens just in time and a very flushed-looking Eline runs in with the dirty dress, which she found at the bottom of a mountain of laundry, at the very back of the laundry room. There's a crumpled white ball in the pocket.

The girl smooths out the card and reads it.

Of course. Now she remembers.

Pierre the footman pours King George and Mr Stiltskin another one. The men drink and look at her standing there with her child in her arms. She still hasn't spoken.

The throne room is blue with cigar smoke. Slowly, the clock ticks towards five.

'Chop, chop,' says the king. 'Just a minor formality, sweetheart. And then we can get on with the rest of our lives.'

She takes a breath.

'All right, then. What's *my* name?' she says.

For a moment, there is silence.

'That's not the point, girl. That's not the question,' says Mr Stiltskin.

'But it's the question I'm asking,' she says. 'Answer me. What's my name?'

'As if you're in any position to be asking the questions here!'

'What's my name?'

'But darling…' the king begins. 'Sweetheart, that wasn't the question. The question is…'

'What am I called? Or don't you know?'

'Of course I do,' says George.

'Oh yes? What is it, then?'

'It's just that… Oh, it's on the tip of my tongue. I, um…'

'Surely you know your own wife's name, George,' giggles Mr Stiltskin.

'Ah, never mind,' the king exclaims. 'I don't always use it, I usually say, um… sweetheart… or… ah, darling… But her father must know it. Maybe I should… Pierre, would you?'

'Well, it must surely be on the marriage certificate too, of course.'

While the men are busily discussing, and footmen are sent to fetch the marriage and birth certificates, the girl gently wraps her child in a blanket. Then she picks up a nappy bag and puts on comfortable shoes, gives Eline a kiss and walks out of the palace.

The forest begins just outside the gate. There are wheat-fields, and fluffy white clouds are floating across the sky. The sun warms her face. The afternoon is soft.

So soft that it seems to be embracing her.

So soft that you could easily reach your hands through it and touch what lies beyond.

WOLF

I

The girl is studying her history book at the kitchen table. The chapter is called 'The Dark Middle Ages'. There is a picture drawn in thick clumsy lines of a man with a black hood on his head. He is swinging a square hammer through the air, and it is about to descend upon another man, who is tied to a big wheel. In the background, two more men are dangling by their necks from the gallows.

Just imagine… the words say. *You are a criminal in the Middle Ages, waiting for a terrible punishment, sweating as you lie awake…*

The history book always says that kind of thing.

Imagine you're a mammoth hunter on the steppe, with only a wooden spear to defend yourself.

Can you imagine how terrified these explorers must have been in the new, unknown world?

'That's good,' her teacher always says. 'It makes history come to life inside your mind.'

The girl looks at the picture for so long and studies it so

closely that she can still see it when she closes her eyes. What a way to go.

'Stupid thing! Why can't you do what you're supposed to?!' Her mother is sitting at the corner of the table, hammering away at the keyboard. 'I only want to get a few groceries delivered to Grandma's. Is that so difficult?'

'Grandma's?' The girl looks up from her book. 'Why?'

'I promised,' says Mum. 'She's ill again. And it always happens whenever I don't have the time to help out.'

'I can go,' says the girl, but her mother isn't listening. She's talking to her screen again. 'Same-day delivery, yeah, yeah. Don't go making promises you can't keep!' She types some more words, refreshes pages. 'Oh yes, of course: too busy. Shall I tell you who's too busy?'

The girl glances up to see if her mother is expecting an answer. It doesn't look like it.

'And I can't go. Not this afternoon.' Her mother sighs and takes a swig from her empty cup. 'Why is that? Why don't I even have time to go and see my own mother when I need to?'

Mum probably isn't expecting an answer this time either. She's hunched at the table as if she's in a shrinking cubicle. She's pulled everything close to her: cups, sheets of paper, a packet of chewing gum so she won't smoke, healthy crackers so she won't put on weight, telephone, laptop, chargers.

The girl looks back at her book. The executioner is still raising his hammer. Any minute now, bones will be shattered, the ones in the arms and the legs first, so the pain lasts extra long. The crowd will cheer every blow. When all the bones are broken, the executioner will finally deliver the death

44

blow. She closes her eyes again. History comes to life inside her mind.

Hit him! the people yell. *Smack! Whack! Show us some blood!*

But that's not going to happen, she thinks. Not in this picture. The executioner will go on swinging his hammer for ever, and the man on the wheel will see the blow coming for all eternity. And he'll be afraid, and maybe he'll scream. But the blow won't come. For a thousand years, he has been frozen in time, looking at a hammer that will never fall.

It doesn't happen. It never happens.

Maybe that's an even worse punishment.

'Come on, you stupid thing! Just do as I say!' Her mother swears, then immediately apologises: 'Sorry.' She always says sorry when she does something she's told herself she's not supposed to do, as if that might erase it. As if the girl doesn't already know all the swear words by now, even the really bad ones. As if she doesn't know that Mum sometimes smokes in secret and drinks an extra glass of wine. As if she cares.

She looks out of the window. It's been raining, but now there are big patches of blue among the grey. If she says she wants to get a breath of fresh air, maybe she'll be allowed. Fresh air is always good for children.

'Why don't I go?' she asks, and this time her mother looks up.

'Go?'

'To Grandma's? With the groceries?'

'Of course you can't go,' her mother says. 'Are you mad? It's much too far.'

He can easily run an entire circuit in one sprint, without getting out of breath. That's good. That means he's still in pretty good condition.

But of course it could also mean that the forest has got smaller again. And in truth, that's what he thinks has happened. Even though that wasn't in the agreement. He doesn't remember everything, but he'd remember that, wouldn't he? Did the forester mention that at all?

It doesn't seem very long since he was last here. But maybe it's been ages.

Seasons. Years.

Doing the same circuit every day sends you crazy in the head. You start seeing things that aren't there. Flashes of prey. Deer darting away, rabbits giggling. Ah, rabbits...

Are we here? Are we there? Bunnies, bunnies everywhere! they chant. *Dozy, tame, way too slow, can you catch us? No, no, no!*

And he starts running, panting, skidding, turning round and round, but all he bites is air. He never catches them.

Because they're not there.

But anyway, that forester. He didn't even take his rifle from his shoulder. His stick just dangled from his belt. Couldn't he have threatened him a little bit? *Back, monster! Back! Or I'll knock the living daylights out of you!* Something along those lines. Even if only out of politeness.

He should have eaten him right there and then. That's what he should have done. He should have waited at first, head down, gazed meekly at the ground, like a tame animal, like a servant. While still keeping a very close eye on everything, every movement, every footstep closer. Ears alert. Muscles tensed in his mighty legs, waiting for the right moment. And then…

And it did come, the right moment. He can still remember exactly when: after the man accidentally turned over two pages of that blasted contract at the same time. And then had to leaf back. And for a second took his eyes off the predator right in front of him.

Then. That's when he should have done it.

One leap, paws on his chest, teeth on his throat. Biting, pulling, tearing. And there his prey would have lain, bleeding and dying, before he understood what had happened. Time to start munching and slurping away. Pawprints in blood on that blasted agreement. And then tearing that up too and trampling it into the mud. Until there was nothing left but steaming flesh in a torn pair of camouflage trousers, and the ground covered in scraps of red.

No more contract. No agreement. No rules. No.

'You can't possibly disagree, sir,' the man had said. Sir – that was something, at least. 'Everything is provided for. All we ask is that you stay within the agreed area. The fence is a sort of reminder. In theory, you could go through it, but I wouldn't if I were you. Not with that transmitter around your neck.'

Not with that what around his what?

It was as if he only really woke up then, only noticed then that they'd been fiddling with him. That they'd attached some-thing around his neck. He shook his head, tried to pull the thing off with his claws, to tear it away, but it stayed put. And when he began running wildly, trying to see if he could get away from it, the beeping started, right in his ear.

The closer he came to the fence, the louder it beeped, wailed, screamed; he held his paws to his ears, heart pounding wildly, but it didn't help. Nothing helped to ease that noise inside his brain. It only stopped when he fled from that fence, further and further away until, exhausted and defeated, his head ringing, he came back to roll at the feet of the forester, who was just standing there. Rifle still on his shoulder. Stick untouched.

'That's what we meant,' the idiot said. 'And that signal? We can hear it too. If it goes on for too long, you can be sure we'll come out immediately and guide you back to the agreed area. I'm assuming we can do that without too much violence. Seriously, we love having you here in our forest. A piece of truly wild nature – that's something we want to preserve. We've already lost so much, haven't we?'

Earnestly, his brown eyes looked down at him. As if they both agreed, as if they both wanted the same thing.

Then, at that moment, that's when he should have torn him apart. Oh, he's so very sorry that he didn't.

Because after that, there was *nothing* to tear apart.

What he receives every day, at exactly the same time, in the agreed place, is long dead. So dead that there's no fun in it any more. At first, he still used to swing it around a bit, roll about with it in the leaves, whining and drooling a little, as if he had to overpower it. But he's stopped doing that now. He eats a bit, but he leaves most of it.

It's not that he isn't hungry any more. He's starving, constantly starving. But not for that sort of junk.

'Just a signature here, please. A pawprint will do,' the forester had said with a smile.

48

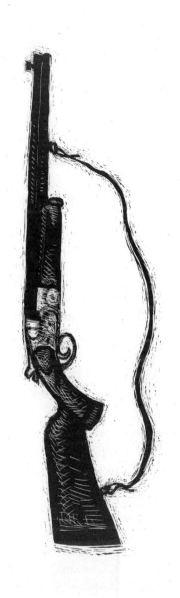

He shook paws with him like a good boy.
And became a slave. A yes-man. A show wolf.

III

Her mother insisted that she wear her fire-red raincoat with
the reflective strips on the arms, back and hood. The girl feels
like a walking traffic light as she heads along the pavement
outside the flats. Plastic bag in one hand, phone in the other.
Everyone can see her, could come dashing out, call the police
at once if anything happens.

But what could happen here?

The paving stones are laid flat and straight, the little gardens neatly fenced in. Even the saplings are strapped firmly
to wooden poles. They can't grow out in every direction, only
straight upwards, just as the town planner intended.

The rain taps on her hood. This isn't really much more fun
than doing homework.

Her phone buzzes in her pocket. *Turn right here.* She does
know the way without that thing, but her mother insisted on
planning the route.

After 500 metres, keep left.

A straight road. Another straight road. Then, after the last
block of flats, she has to carry straight on, past the cemetery.

'You won't be too scared, will you?' her mother asked.
'I could always take you. It should be fine, actually.'

'There's no need, Mum. Really.'

'But I don't want you to go into the cemetery. Okay?'

'Can't I just wave at Grandpa?'

'From a distance. Don't go through the gate.'

'Okay, from a distance.'

Behind the fence, dead people lie in straight lines under thick slabs of marble. She's forgotten where her grandpa is – all the graves look alike. For a moment, the girl considers just waving, but the gate is already wide open, as if inviting her in. She could just walk straight in.

The second row, she thinks. No, the third. Her boots crunch over the gravel.

Everyone here is just a name now, carved into the shiny stone. *Beloved father. Taken from us too soon. Safe in Jesus's arms.* Born, died, born, died. Upright in the rain or flat and covered with puddles.

Towards the back, the stones are more crooked, moss-covered and illegible.

Is this place haunted? Not now, in daylight with the roar of the main road nearby, but maybe on a moonless night? As the ground begins to shake, an eerie violin begins to play and the tombstones begin to move to the beat of the music… As a dead claw works its way up through the earth, a coffin lid slowly opens and something rises, something that has been gnawed at by the worms, something that gazes out of empty sockets, something that…

Ah, yes. Just like the haunted house at the fair. She once spent an hour in there, and on a ten-minute cycle she saw the same ghosts appear, the same hand lifting the same lid, to the accompaniment of the same jingling music. Throughout it all, she could hear the squeaking of the machinery. After the sixth cycle, the lid got stuck, and that was the most exciting thing that happened. But a man came running up with a toolbox, and she wasn't allowed to stay and watch but had to go back outside with the crowd of people.

It doesn't say anywhere how these dead people died, whether it was in agony, after terrible suffering, or a horrific accident. Maybe even a murder? She has to fill in the gaps herself.

Her grandpa once took her to the church he sometimes went to. Bleeding hearts everywhere, saints riddled with arrows, cramped hands with nails right through them – she stared and stared. She wouldn't have suspected it of her dull grandpa.

She wanted to go again, but Mum wouldn't let her. 'I'm glad I'm out of it,' she said. 'Please don't get involved with that nonsense.'

Grandpa died just as he had lived: in his chair, holding his newspaper. Did anyone cry for him? Grandma told herself to be brave and to keep going. Mum seemed relieved more than anything.

As for herself, she did her best. *Oh, Grandpa…* she wrote in her diary. *My dear grandpa, I can't live without him, I'm going to mourn him for ever and ever…*

But even as she was writing it, she knew that was rubbish. Nothing bad had happened, not really.

Oh look, there he is, lying under his pink stone. She reads his name and his dates.

'Oh, Grandpa…' she says, trying to sigh mournfully.

The telephone buzzes. *Are you there yet?*

IV

Beep beep beepbeepbeeeeeep…
   It's driving him crazy.

'We'll come out immediately to guide you back to the agreed area,' they had said.

But he doesn't see anyone coming. A bit closer to the fence?

Beepbeepbeepbeeeep… No one.

Is this what he wants?

Yes, blast it, he thinks that it is.

All day long, he has had mischief on his mind. And hunger in his stomach, but not for that limp, dead meat. For something alive, something struggling. Something afraid.

Let them come, he thinks. All of them at once if necessary, with nets and sticks, with fire. He will fight them. Let them shoot! He knows what it's like to be hit by buckshot, he's not afraid of that. It stings, burns for a bit, but he can bite it out – and he'll just have to do with a missing chunk of flesh from his flank. He is a wolf, not a scared sheep. So, he'll just have to limp for a while.

But… they don't use buckshot any more. They shoot with something meaner than that, and it feels like just a little prick. But then he loses himself. His head fills with sludge, his thoughts melt, the darkness pulls him in. And when, much later, he has fought his way back out, he feels sick and giddy and angry. And his legs don't work any more. He really doesn't want to go through all that again.

He steps back from the fence. Better not, not today.

The beeping dies down, and he can hear his thoughts again.

What are you? they say. A dishrag? A sheep? Who says it'll be the same this time? Scaredy cat. Lazy lapdog. Maybe it'll be different today. Maybe this is your lucky day, Wolf. You're not going to let it get away, are you? Maybe you can run from tree

to tree, avoid the jabs, and then, when they come after you, you can lure them to the pit you dug, remember? With the sticks around to make them trip? Maybe they'll get caught, maybe they'll go down, rifles falling from their hands, chins hitting the edge, and before they know what's happening, you'll be on their necks and biting into the soft…

No, no, that's not allowed. You shook paws, remember? You're a show wolf, that's the agreement. That's why you can stay. Otherwise they'll stuff you with wool and send you to a museum as 'educational material' – he can still see the word written in the contract in pointed black letters. Keep to the agreement, be a wolf of your word, be a…

To hell with his word! His word would be enough to hold him back every other day, but not today.

Today is different. Today he's had enough. He's had more than enough.

Today smells of adventure.

He howls, he wails, he runs. His collar beeps like crazy, but so what? Let them come, let it happen. Just let something happen. Anything. Not nothing. He's sick of that nothing, sick to the back teeth.

V

Something is howling in the forest.

The girl stops to listen. What was it?

Of course it can't be what it sounds like. Probably just a dog whose tail has been stepped on, in a neat garden, attached

56

to a newbuild house on an estate somewhere. Maybe even a funny ringtone.

Not a wolf, though – it can't be that.

But still, she can hear it. There it is again.

She looks around. The sky is grey, the rain is drizzling down, the dead people are lying dead still in their neat little gardens. But as the howling continues, the world around her expands, the forest in the distance grows taller and darker.

There's something there. There really is something there.

It *is* a wolf.

At the back of the cemetery is a hedge she can get through. Beyond that, the forest begins. A ditch runs around it, and then there's a fence with seven taut strands of barbed wire. *No trespassing*, the wire says. *Forbidden. Danger. Turn around. Go away.*

She walks on. The hedge makes a bit of an effort to stop her, but she pushes the branches aside.

Her telephone buzzes again, but she ignores it.

She steps into the ditch. Her boots sink into mud and leaves. The bag of groceries snags on something and tears. The packet of chocolate biscuits falls into the mud. But she doesn't pick it up. She just trudges on.

The barbed wire looms over the edge of the ditch. The trees beyond are dark, their branches pointing up like dead fingers, and there's that howling again. Much closer now.

She pulls herself up and looks through the fence.

There. She can see it.

Something is running from tree to tree, lower than a human being, much faster too. Paws drumming, leaves flying up. She hears panting – and something quietly beeping.

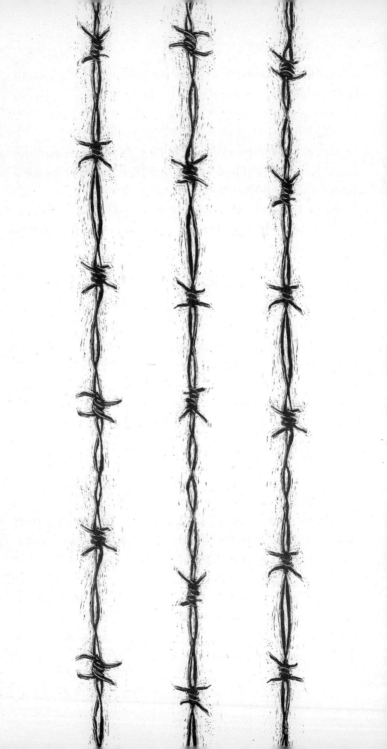

Her breathing quickens, and she grabs the taut wire with both hands. There are spikes on it that could give her a nasty jab, but so what?

There he is.

He's bigger than any dog she's ever seen. His fur is grey and black, his eyes are yellow, and out of his mouth comes a red tongue that keeps flashing across his lips.

He looks like a wolf, and he smells of wolf. Their eyes lock.

Turn around, buzzes the telephone in her pocket. *Return to your planned route!*

VI

Well, how about that? So, that was what he could smell.

It's prey. That's what it is. Prey! Over there! So close! Not a rabbit, something else, a little human, a girl, red as blood, with soft flesh and slow feet. The drool comes running from his mouth when he sees it and smells it: young, defenceless, sweet. And his for the taking. His jaws open and close, his tongue flicks over his teeth as if he can already taste that redness, all that redness over there.

He takes a step closer to the fence. And another.

But oh, the beeping! The beeping! It's a deafening racket inside his head. It seems to make his predator brain smaller, more afraid. His legs stiffen – and stop.

Go on! he shouts at himself. Push through the wire, seize that prey! You can't miss, your belly will be full, your head will go wild, you'd be a fool to let this one get away…

Yes, but the beeping. Yes, but the forester. Yes, but the jab, the wool, the educational material…

His head is driving him crazy, and he cringes and cowers.

He stands there, and she stands there, with the fence between them.

VII

The wolf behind the wire crouches down.

Preparing to jump, she thinks – and closes her eyes.

One more second. One more second, and then she'll start screaming, high and loud, so it'll cut through the forest, she'll turn and run, with the monster after her. For now, the fence is holding him back, but the strands of wire are wide apart, he can squeeze through them, she hears his paws drumming closer, and she runs. He doesn't have her yet, but it won't be long. She throws away the plastic bag, the bottle breaks, red wine comes gushing out, and she runs, she runs through the ditch, through the hedge, she feels his warm breath on the back of her neck and she runs, gravel spraying high.

They go straight across the cemetery. Maybe this is where he'll catch her, in the middle of the graves, and she can stay there and what remains of her can go into the ground in a little white coffin, next to Grandpa, so sad, so beautiful, so…

She opens her eyes again.

He is still exactly where he was. A little further away than before, it seems.

'Hello?' The girl rattles the barbed wire. 'So… are you coming after me or not?'

VIII

He takes a step forward and a step back. Forward and back and again and again. He spins around like a rabid dog.

'What are you waiting for?' she says.

What is he waiting for?

He sees a small hand coming through the barbed wire. A pointed barb snags and tears a cut in her skin. He smells blood. He's going crazy.

'Are you scared? Is that it?'

Scared? Him? Of course not. How ridiculous.

Yes, he's scared.

Back and forth. Back and forth again. The beeping shrieks in his ear. He can still see her. It's still possible.

But when he puts a paw on the fence, sirens begin to blare in the distance. They're coming, he knew it. He shrinks, runs from tree to tree, away, he has to get away, has to hide, in a place where their needles can't touch him, at the bottom of the trap maybe, if he makes himself small, very small and invisible.

'Coward!' he hears her shouting. 'What kind of wolf are you?'

Not a wolf, he is not a wolf.

IX

Brakes screeching, the van stops by the hedge. Men jump out and run across the ditch with big strides. They have hats and large guns. One-two-three and they're beside her. The girl is grabbed under the armpits and carried away. Two of them put her into the van, four head into the forest, sticks in hand.

'Are you out of your mind, child?' the two men cry. 'What were you doing there?'

'You could have died. You do realise that, don't you?'

The girl doesn't say anything, just squeezes her hand. Droplets of blood seep out between her fingers.

'Oh my God!' the foresters gasp. 'It's bitten her!' They open a first-aid kit, take out plasters and iodine and large rolls of gauze.

'No, no, that wasn't…' the girl says. 'It was the…' But they're already rolling up her sleeve and dabbing her wrist.

'This might sting for a moment. Grit your teeth!'

'But there's no need,' she protests. 'He didn't…'

'Of course there is. Bites like this can get badly infected.'

'He didn't…'

'Maybe tetanus, too?'

'Yes, definitely tetanus.'

He didn't do anything, she wants to say, it was the barbed wire. But no one is listening. She can't even see her cut now, with so much gauze and cotton wool wrapped around it.

'Your mother's already on her way in the car.'

'Such a fright for her. The poor woman.'

'Just be glad it turned out so well.'

'Yeah, I've been saying it for ages. It's a stupid idea, so close to a residential area.'

'Completely irresponsible.'

'They really need to put a stop to it. We're going to have to…' says the one.

'Yes, it's a shame,' says the other. 'But you're right, we really are.'

They nod and dab and wrap more gauze around her.

After a while, the other four return to the van. One of them is carrying her torn plastic bag. The others are dragging something behind them: something big and black and limp.

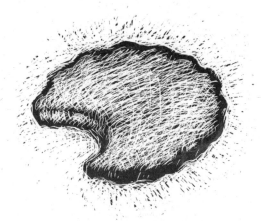

BISCUITS

The girls had lost their mother. She had died a few months ago, in a white hospital.

Luckily, they still had a father. But he was spending more and more time away from home. He was late more and more often, sometimes so late that they were almost asleep when he got home. Very quietly, he would slip into their bedroom and sit down on the edge of the bed.

'I have to do this – just for a while,' he whispered to his daughters on their pillows. 'A big new project. You do understand, don't you?' The girls nodded, too sleepy to hear what exactly it was that they were supposed to understand, but they knew their father really wanted them to. Because when everything in your life has collapsed, you have to hold on to something, and work was what their father chose to hold on to.

'But everything's fine, isn't it?' he said when he briefly saw them in the morning at breakfast. 'You're my big, brave girls, right?'

And then the girls nodded and smiled as bravely as they could.

Greta was the older of the two, so she had to be the sensible one. Their father always gave her the money for the shopping.

'Get some milk and vegetables, eh?' he said, still munching, as he put his coat back on. 'Got to get your vitamins. Oh, but you know all about that, don't you?'

And yes, Greta did know all about that. But when life has had a hole punched in it, you have to fill that hole with something, and vitamins don't do much to help. So, she bought wine gums with the money, and liquorice and marshmallows and fizzy pop and cookies and, if there was any money left, she also bought an apple for Hanna, her sister.

Hanna didn't like sweets. Which was just as well, because Greta rarely left any. She put the shopping bag on the table, without even unpacking, and ate until it was empty. She often ate the apple too. And then she cried, because she had stomach ache and was full of guilt and regret now that the food was all gone, but mostly because of her mother, of course.

Hanna used to comfort her. She said that tomorrow would be better. That Dad would come home earlier, would stay longer and that the three of them would do something fun together: go to see a film or to the swimming pool or just sit at the table and play cards. And every morning, she asked her dad to do exactly that. He nodded. Yes, definitely. Just not today.

'Soon,' he said. 'Tomorrow. Or next week at the latest.'

'Really? Next week? You promise? Hand on your heart?' Hanna took her father's hand and got him to promise.

Because when so much of what has always been there disappears, you have to hold on to something, and Hanna held on tightly to her sister with one hand and to her father with the other. But his grip was becoming looser and looser, as if there were soapy suds on his hand, and after a few weeks of promises broken over and over again, he slipped away.

He didn't come home. One evening. Two nights. Three.

'What if he never comes back?' wailed Greta, chewing on the last apple core. The money was gone, the bread bin was empty and all there was in the pantry was a jar of gherkins.

'Of course he's coming back.' Hanna nodded, as if she were sure of that.

'And if he doesn't?'

'Then we'll just have to come up with some way to find food.'

'Like what?'

'Something clever.'

So, the very next morning, they started swapping toys at school. The girls had a lot of nice things at home; their father had always been more generous with gifts than he was with himself. And the other children in their class were only too happy to swap.

'We'd rather have money, but food's okay too,' said Hanna. All of the children chose food.

The contents of lunchboxes for Lego trains, Barbie dolls or expensive teddy bears – that wasn't a bad exchange. Hanna didn't mind. She didn't care much about things. Greta found it more difficult, but having no food is worse than having no toys. Before long, their bedroom was empty, except for their two beds.

'There are some other things we could swap…' said Hanna then, and she and Greta lugged it all to school. The TV, the lamps, the dining-room chairs…

The children in their class soon got used to it, and so did their parents. They gave their children extra lunch to take to school.

'And make sure you drive a hard bargain,' they said. 'It'll be good experience for later in life.'

The teacher saw what was happening, but he thought it was some kind of game and didn't object. He only drew the line when the girls brought in a big grandfather clock on their scooter.

'You can't bring that into the classroom, kids,' he said when they shakily dragged the thing through the door. 'Who does it belong to?'

'Me, sir!' said the richest boy in the class, putting his hand up. 'Swapped for it.'

'Is that so?'

The sisters nodded. He had given them a packet of pink-iced biscuits for it, which Hanna had quickly slipped into her bag. Otherwise they would have soon disappeared. She helped the boy to roll the clock back out into the corridor.

'The scooter, too,' the boy said. 'Or the deal's off.'

Hanna just nodded.

'Now don't go bringing anything else like that in with you,' said the teacher, and the girls obediently shook their heads.

Anyway, they had nothing to bring – their home was empty. In the kitchen, only the table was left, because they couldn't get it through the door. It was covered with bills and brightly coloured brochures and leaflets full of things they would never be able to buy.

And their father still hadn't come back.

The sisters had to try very hard not to cry when they came home to their empty flat that afternoon. Hanna sat down on the table, Greta on the floor.

'Hey, give me those biscuits,' she said.

'No.' Hanna shook her head. 'We're going to do something else with them.'

The biscuits were so terribly pink that it hurt your eyes. Hanna broke one in two and put half on the pavement opposite their flat, at the foot of a traffic light. She took her sister to the end of the street. When they looked back, they could easily see the patch of pink lying there.

'We're going to look for Dad,' she said. 'And if we put half a biscuit on the ground every time we turn a corner, we'll always be able to find our way back. Good plan, huh?'

Greta looked hesitantly at the packet. Written on it in pink and gold letters was *Sweet Mothers' Biscuits*. She wanted one so much that she could hardly think about anything else.

'Nitwit,' she said. 'The birds will eat them right up.'

'No, they won't, nitwit.' Hanna had already walked on, almost as far as the corner. 'There aren't any birds in the city.'

'Nitwit yourself,' said Greta tagging along after her sister. 'And what if it rains? Then they'll wash away.'

'No, they won't, nitwit. It's not going to rain.'

That was indeed how it looked: the sky was bright blue, as it had been all week. Just the kind of weather to go swimming with your dad, if you had one. Or to fill the paddling pool on the balcony, if it was still there.

'But, but…' Greta looked around. The city stretched away from the girls in all directions. 'We have no idea where…'

'Of course we do, nitwit. We've been there, haven't we?' That was true. When their mum was still alive, they sometimes went to meet Dad from work, as a surprise.

'I'm sure we'll recognise it,' Hanna said firmly. 'It was a grey office block. How difficult can it be?'

She placed half a biscuit at the foot of a lamppost. 'We'll go left here.'

Greta looked down at the pink half-moon and sighed.

'Okay, then,' she said. 'But I'll be the one who leaves the bits of biscuit behind.'

Hanna hesitated for a moment, but then passed the packet to her sister.

It was much harder than they'd imagined. The city was big and noisy and complicated, and they soon lost count of the grey office blocks they had seen where no one answered the door or where the doorman sent the girls packing. No one knew their father.

They laid a slow trail through the city. They stood on the pavement and waited for every light to change, just as they had been taught. But their feet were starting to hurt and their stomachs were cramping with hunger. At least, Hanna's was.

'You are leaving the bits of biscuit on the ground, aren't you?' she said anxiously to Greta a few times.

Greta nodded angrily. 'Yes, I am! Don't you trust me?'

'Of course I do.'

'I'm the big sister. I'm the responsible one.' With an angry snap, Greta broke another biscuit in two. When she saw that Hanna wasn't looking, she quickly popped it into her mouth. She truly had been determined not to eat them all herself. But as often happened with things she was determined not to do, she did it anyway. Quietly, she sucked on the pink sugar, so that Hanna wouldn't hear the crunch.

'I think we're almost there,' Hanna kept saying. 'I'm sure I'm starting to recognise things now.' And so they would walk along another street full of grey office blocks, ring another bell, get sent away again – and it was starting to get dark.

'Let's go home,' decided Hanna. 'Tomorrow is another day. We can finish the gherkins for dinner.' She was so hungry that it suddenly didn't sound like such a bad idea. 'Where did you leave the last bit of biscuit?'

Greta looked at the ground and crumpled the empty packet in her fist.

Hanna had got terribly angry. And Greta had got terribly angry too. They had called each other all kinds of bad names and had both said that they were leaving and that the other one could suit herself and do whatever she liked, but when they'd wiped their tears and their noses on the sleeves of their T-shirts, they were still standing next to each other in the rapidly darkening, unfamiliar street. What else could they do but stay together?

So, they just started walking again, going around and around in circles.

The people who passed them didn't look at the girls. Or they *did* look, and then the two girls walked on very quickly, heads down, staring at their feet.

'I can't go any further, Hanna…' Greta stopped, in the middle of the pavement. 'I really can't. I really can't.' She started crying.

'Yes, you can. Just a bit longer. We're nearly there.'

'You keep saying that. And it's still not true.'

'Yes, it is, really, honestly… I… You did put some bits of biscuit down to start with, didn't you? I think I can smell one.'

'Nitwit, that's impossible, with all these exhaust fumes,' Greta was about to say, but now she could smell it too: a delicious, vaguely sweet scent. Following their noses, the girls turned the corner. There, in the next street, a soft-pink light shone from a shop window. *Sweet Mothers' Biscuits* it said, in pink and gold letters in an arc on the glass. Behind the glass, the biscuits were stacked high.

Like a hungry moth, Greta fluttered towards the light and rested her head on the window. The shop had closed hours ago, and of course the girls had no money. But she didn't want to walk any more. She just wanted to look at the biscuits.

'Oh, that little bottom lip…' said someone. 'Ah, just look at that!'

'That little pout, those longing eyes…' said someone else. 'So sweet!'

'So cute!'

'Couldn't you just eat her right up?!'

Three ladies had appeared in the window, round and pink, with blond plaits. They were smiling and nodding at Greta

74

and reaching out their arms to her, as if they wanted to give her a cuddle through the glass.

The door was already opening and, along with the scent of biscuits, sweet voices came drifting out towards the sisters in the dark evening.

'Come on, come on in, girls. Quickly!'

Greta was already standing in the doorway.

'Please. Do we have to?' Hanna said quietly. But she had no idea where else to go, so she followed her sister into the warm shop.

It was like walking right into heaven. The shop smelled delicious, as if the air itself were made of warm milk, with sugar and a dash of cinnamon, just like their mother used to make when they couldn't sleep. Their stomachs felt empty and their heads could only think about food. As if they were sleepwalking, the sisters followed the pink ladies.

The ladies bustled all around the girls, to the front and the back and the sides, taking Greta by the hand and sitting her down on a soft stool in the middle of the shop. They brought plates full of biscuits, and steaming cups, and cameras.

'Tuck in!' they said. 'Take a bite!'

One lady held up a biscuit close to her face. Greta was about to grab it, but the lady pulled it away.

'No, no, first do that lip again. For the camera.'

'Lip?' asked Greta.

'That sad bottom lip. That pout. Yes, go on!'

'As if the biscuit is the one thing you want most in the whole world.'

That wasn't difficult – because that was exactly how it felt. Longingly, Greta reached out her hand.

'Yes, yes, like that! That's what we mean!' They took photos of Greta, lots of photos. All the flashes made her a bit dizzy.

'Hey, what are you doing with my sister?' asked Hanna, who was still standing by the door.

'Ah, she's jealous,' giggled the pink ladies. 'Do you want to sit on the stool too? You can have a go in a minute.'

'Not really,' said Hanna. 'But could I just use the phone for a moment?'

'Of course,' said the Sweet Mothers. 'When we're finished.'

First, Greta had to grab the biscuit again, and then again with her other hand, and once again with her hair neatly combed, and then she was finally allowed to have the biscuit. She took a big bite.

'Oh, that smile!' the Sweet Mothers cooed. 'Those cute little round cheeks!'

Flash and click went the cameras again.

'That was tasty, eh? Wasn't that the most delicious biscuit in the whole world?'

Greta nodded, a little stunned, but it was true. And she wanted another one.

'No, first another smile. Happy, happy. Yes, like that, and… hold it!'

The cameras flashed on all sides, the ladies squeezed her cheeks and waved more biscuits around to get her attention.

'Here! Look over here! That's right. Can you be even more… radiant? No, don't look at your sister. She can have a turn in a minute.'

When they'd taken a hundred photographs of Greta, Hanna was allowed to sit on the stool. She did want a biscuit, but she didn't want to smile.

'Go on,' the ladies said. 'Just like your sister. Happy, happy!'

'But I'm not happy,' said Hanna. She cast a worried glance through the window, where night had fallen. If their father came home this evening, they wouldn't be there.

'Not happy? What child isn't happy with a Sweet Mothers' Biscuit? Go on! Take a bite!'

But Hanna wasn't much good to them. When she was allowed to have the biscuit, she only took a little nibble.

'Delicious, eh? So, so tasty?'

'Um, yes,' she said politely. 'Very tasty. Do you think I could have an apple?'

'An apple?' The Sweet Mothers sighed in surprise. What kind of child actually volunteers to eat an apple?

They chased the strange girl off the stool and put Greta back onto it. They cuddled her and gave her bites and sips, and the girl couldn't stop chewing and swallowing and smiling because of everything that she'd missed for so long and now suddenly had so much of.

'Do you have a computer I could use?' asked Hanna. 'And a telephone?'

'Why?' asked the pink ladies warily. 'Who do you want to call?'

'My dad.' Hanna gulped. 'But I don't know his number, and… and he hasn't come home, and…'

'Not for ages!' Greta started crying.

'Oh, you poor little orphans!' cried the mothers. 'Abandoned and forgotten! All alone in the big, bad city…' They looked at one another for a moment from under their beautifully curled eyelashes.

'That's not true!' cried Hanna. 'He's coming back. Tomorrow or the next day or…'

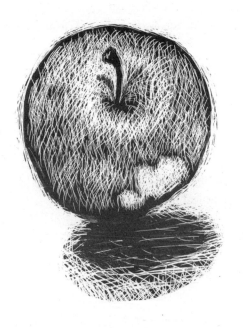

'Or never, ever again!' sobbed Greta.

'Poor, poor children,' the Sweet Mothers sighed. 'What a terrible man!'

No, he isn't, Hanna wanted to shout, but her sister was crying so loudly now that no one could hear anything else.

'It's so lucky we found you,' the mothers said soothingly. 'It's so lucky that you're here now, where it's warm and safe. And you can stay for as long as you like. We'll take a few more photos tomorrow, yes? We'll bring in a hairdresser. And we'll do some different outfits. Won't that be fun?'

'But…' Hanna whispered. 'My dad. I need to…'

'All in good time, all in good time.' The Sweet Mothers stroked Greta and tried to kiss Hanna. 'Tomorrow. Or the day after. We'll see. First have a good night's sleep.' They gently pushed the girls into a little room with two beds. The pillows were pink. The sheets were pink. The girls were so tired that they dropped straight onto the mattresses.

'But we are *not* staying,' said Hanna when the mothers had closed the door. 'If you ask me, they're witches.'

'Nitwit,' said Greta, her head snuggled warmly into the pillow. 'Witches aren't pink.'

In his grey office, high above the city, Hanna and Greta's father was sitting at his desk. He was squeezing his phone so hard that it almost hurt. After that last call, when the very last deal was sealed, it felt as if he'd just woken from a long dream full of lots of big bucks and wheeling and dealing.

Suddenly… he remembered that he had two daughters. That he was the one person who was supposed to be looking after them. And that he'd abandoned them for over a week. When he looked more closely at his diary, he saw that it was actually more like two weeks. So, he decided not to look quite so closely.

Had he really forgotten about them? For all that time?

While everyone in his department was congratulating one another on the fantastic result and people kept coming over to slap him on the back, he just sat there on his chair.

His mind was racing.

Not because he was trying to think what he should do. He knew that already. Go home, right now, sort everything out, make sure his girls were safe and then apologise a hundred million times for being such a bad father. He had to do that right away. He couldn't wait another second.

But he didn't stand up and head to the door. Because when you've done something really terrible, it's not always easy to admit it. It's simpler to imagine that maybe it wasn't that bad after all and that there really were good reasons for doing what you did.

Yes, it was bad, but… His mind whirred. I was confused. I was in mourning. I couldn't help it.

Yes, but… I really did think about you a lot, but I was busy making money, for the two of you, for all of us. Someone has to do that, don't they?

Yes, but I… His mind went on whirring, and then: But what about you two?!

You never said anything. Or called me, or anything like that. You had my number, didn't you?

Or did they? Had he actually ever given it to them? He squeezed the phone so hard that he almost crushed it. He really should have given them the number.

Yes, but… his head began again, I was confused, I was in mourning. Yes, but… Yes, but…

He had to leave. Now. At once.

But instead he just sat there, with the telephone in his hand. Inside his head, his daughters were crying their eyes out, screaming with anger, or starving to death.

If he'd looked out of the window, he would have seen one of his daughters, on a large billboard, high above the houses. The Sweet Mothers had moved quickly with their latest advertising campaign. With gleaming eyes and a sweet, pouting lip, Greta gazed at the biscuit in her hand.

Give your child the best! it said, in pink and gold letters. *Give them a Sweet Mothers' Biscuit!*

But he didn't look out of the window.

The Sweet Mothers had eventually locked Hanna in the kitchen. At least she could make herself useful there. She had squirmed her way out of every pink dress and refused to smile nicely for the camera. So, now she was responsible for sliding the baking trays into the oven, pressing the button and, when the bell rang, taking them back out, putting the pink icing on the biscuits and popping them into packets.

They'd already plucked her out from behind the computer ten times. She kept going over there and tapping on the keyboard and asking to use the telephone, and that was simply not allowed. All in good time, the Sweet Mothers said. When the time came. But now was never a good time.

Anyway, why was she complaining? Hadn't they given her a beautiful Barbie doll too? Even though it was Greta who did all the work? Well, then. Why couldn't she be happy and grateful? Why couldn't she be sweet and cooperative, like her sister?

What a success her sister had been! They'd taken one wonderful photo of her after another, enough to sell their biscuits to all the children in the country. And to their parents of course, because a child who looks so happy, who smiles so sweetly, who is so completely and utterly contented – that's what every good parent wants.

'You've stopped trying – and we think that's a shame,' the Sweet Mothers said to Greta, not very sweetly. 'That smile could be a lot wider and a lot happier. Do we need to remind you what you were like when you came here? Hungry, dirty, tears running down your cheeks? Do you remember? Well, that gratitude is what we want to see again.'

'Take another biscuit,' they said. 'Brush the crumbs off your mouth. Careful with your make-up!'

'And now stop eating, please,' they said. 'You're not getting any thinner, you know, and no one ever made a good advertisement with fat girls, as I'm sure you can imagine. All right then, just one more.'

Greta tried to listen to all three of the voices at once, tried to suck in her stomach, to keep her tears inside, and not to move her head too much so that she wouldn't pull out her tightly woven fake plaits.

She looked at the biscuit in front of her face. Had she ever really liked them?

'Taste it on your tongue!' cooed the pink mothers. 'Smell that delicious scent!'

But it didn't smell delicious at all. It smelled of burned biscuit mixture and melted plastic. And there was smoke coming through the crack of the kitchen door.

'Something's wrong with the oven!' screamed Hanna. 'Can I come out of the kitchen for a minute, please? Can I phone the fire brigade?'

Startled, the Sweet Mothers rushed into the kitchen. Dirty black smoke was billowing from the oven, and a whole batch of biscuits was burned black. And who on earth had put that Barbie doll on the baking tray?

Behind their backs, Hanna slipped into the office, typed her father's name and pressed 'Search'.

And she searched and searched and searched.

As he opened the front door, Hanna and Greta's father saw that it was far worse than he'd feared.

He'd finally stood up from his chair, walked out of his office, down the stairs, faster and faster, until he was leaping down several steps at once, and then he'd run all the way home, without stopping, leaving behind a trail of honking traffic, and now he was standing, panting and gasping for breath, upstairs in the flat.

The place was empty. Everything was gone, except for the dining table. The girls... His knees gave way when he thought about his girls. He should call the police. Now. But he didn't dare.

How long? they would say. *What kind of worthless father leaves his children for a whole week... Two?!*

We sent them on to the child protection agency a few days ago, they would say. *Don't imagine you'll ever see them again. And it's what you deserve. Monster.*

In the bare bedroom, there was one of Greta's pillows, and the blanket still smelled a bit like Hanna. He curled up underneath it. Just for a moment, he told himself. Just to work up some courage, and then he would go and face it all and sort everything out. Really.

His telephone woke him up. An unknown number. A client? Not now! He rejected the call twice before answering.

'Yes, what?' he snapped. 'Who? The fire brigade? This isn't the number of the…'

'Daddy?' whispered Hanna on the other end of the line. 'Have I finally found you?'

'Just one more!' the Sweet Mothers cried when the burned biscuits and the melted Barbie had been disposed of and Hanna was mopping up the water they'd used to put the fire out. 'This is all taking far, far too much time. We can't waste an entire day. Sit down! Sit down and smile!'

They planted Greta on the stool again, with her dress and her plaits and the biscuit in front of her nose. And Greta was sick of it, but she didn't dare to say so and she was doing her best to smile one more time, as happily as she could, when she spotted something through the shop window, outside on the street.

'Oh! Yes! Like that!' the Mothers chorused. 'That's exactly what we mean. That's perfect. Hold it!'

And they clicked and flashed, but the girl stood up and ran to the door. 'Daddy!' she sobbed happily.

Behind the kitchen door, someone shouted exactly the same thing.

'Not another single second on TV,' declared Father, who was glad that he could finally seem like a responsible parent again. 'Or in the newspapers. Not anywhere. I do not give my permission for anything.'

'But the money…' sighed the Sweet Mothers. 'If we give you five per cent of every…'

Father shook his head very firmly.

'Ten per cent? Twenty?'

'Nope. And count yourselves lucky that I'm not calling the police!'

Hanna and Greta beamed up at their sensible father, who had no plans ever to tell the police about any of this. He led his two daughters outside.

The Sweet Mothers watched from the pink shop as they walked down the street, the girls skipping alongside their father. Not one of the three looked back.

'Daddy…' Hanna took hold of her father's hand. 'From now, will you stay… Will you never go away for so long again?'

Once more, her father shook his head very firmly. 'Never again,' he said.

'Will you always stay with us? Do you promise?'

'Always,' her father said. 'Although…' he continued. 'We do need, um, obviously… I don't know exactly what you did with the furniture, but we do need some new stuff and, um, someone will obviously have to…'

'But this week,' said Hanna. 'All this week you'll stay at home.'

Her father nodded again. 'Of course. All this week.'

They walked along the pavement in silence for a while.

'Well, in any case…' he said. 'At least tomorrow. Hand on my heart.'

The girls looked at each other. Greta gave a little sigh.

'But everything went okay without me there, didn't it?' He ruffled the girls' hair. 'It went really well, my big, brave girls! Right, so what are we going to do? How about a film? Or a nice meal?'

But the girls weren't interested. All they wanted to do was to go home. Even though there weren't any lights left or any dining chairs. Because when you're that happy to be together again, you don't mind sitting on the floor in the dark.

'How about getting a nice takeaway, then?'

'Not hungry,' said Greta.

'And we still have the gherkins,' said Hanna with a smile. She gave her dad's hand a squeeze with one hand and took her sister's hand in the other. She held them so tightly that it almost hurt.

FROG

The girl is obviously still very grateful to him for fishing her golden ball out of the pond. And of course, he was allowed to sit at the table with her after that and to eat food from her plate and eventually she even let him sleep in her bed with her. At first, she lay right at the edge of the bed so she touched him as little as possible, but when they rolled together into the middle of the bed in the night, she finally went and gave him a kiss, with her eyes squeezed shut and her lips pushed out as far as she could. It wasn't nearly as disgusting as she'd imagined.

But it didn't change anything either.

'Maybe once isn't enough…' he croaked. So, she kissed him a few more times.

'Maybe you need to do it with more enthusiasm. You have to really mean it. Or it won't work.'

She did her best to really mean it. Was as enthusiastic as she could be.

'I feel pretty bad about it too,' he said. 'I'm sure it's my fault.' He looked very sad. 'Maybe I just need more time.'

They let a few days go by. And then a few more. Kept setting the alarm clock for an hour later, and when it went off, they kissed. Then they waited together, as patiently as they could. But nothing happened.

'Well, now I feel like I have to do it!' he said. 'Which makes it impossible to do it. Stop pressuring me!'

She tried not to pressure him.

Meanwhile he ate whatever was served every day and drank beer with her father in the two big armchairs by the fireplace. They told each other jokes and had burping contests. He helped her mother with the washing up as well as he could, with that big tea towel in his little hands. Sometimes he dived in among the cups in the water. That always made her jump, and she couldn't help laughing at the funny little creature.

And every afternoon he spent a long time in the bath. He said it helped.

'I can feel that I'm really starting to change now, sweet-heart,' he would say. 'Can you see it?'

The girl would nod. 'Yes, perhaps a little.'

She really tried to see it, too. But she didn't see it.

And it didn't happen.

He was a frog.

A frog.

A frog.

'But a nice frog, eh?' said her mother. 'I wouldn't worry about it too much.'

'I don't want a frog, though,' said the girl. 'I want him to turn into a prince. That's what he promised.'

'Ah, men promise all kinds of things…' Her mother gave a sigh, glancing at the door. 'But if you really can't get used to it… Go and talk to my sister. She's very wise.'

'Hmm…' The girl's aunt poured her a cup of green tea. 'A frog is a frog. There's not much to be done about that.'

'But I don't want a frog,' said the girl.

'Fine. Then there are a couple of possibilities. Perhaps he suddenly changes one day after all… It's not very likely. But it's possible. You *have* kissed him enough, haven't you?'

The girl nodded.

'From front to back, from left to right?'

'Oh yes,' said the girl.

'And what was it like?'

What was it like? A failure, she wanted to say. After every kiss, she had opened her eyes and, once again, not seen what she had hoped to see. But the kissing itself? Wide-mouthed. Green. Soft, too. The rest of him was far too small, of course, but his mouth – his mouth was just right.

'What's that little smile about?' asked her aunt, who always saw everything.

The girl shrugged.

'Well, yes, there's always that possibility as well,' said her aunt. 'That you get used to him. Having a frog as a husband has disadvantages, but there are certainly advantages, too.'

'Yes, but… I wanted a prince.'

'Ah, a prince, a prince… Have you ever seen a prince up close?'

The girl shook her head. 'But I know they're not green,' she said, as she was very certain of that.

'Most of them aren't. That's true.'

'And they're not so small, with such big, wide mouths.'

'Ah, you see all sorts out there,' her aunt said, cheerfully

blowing on her tea. 'But fine, if you really can't get over it…
then one of you will have to go.'

'Go?'

'And I'd say it should be you.'

'Me?'

Her aunt nodded. 'Men – I mean, frogs – are pretty attached
to their homes.'

'But…' The girl hadn't been expecting that. 'Isn't there
a… I thought, um… maybe a spell or a pill or something?'

'There aren't any pills for that sort of thing,' said her aunt.
'No pills, no shortcuts. Life isn't a fairy tale, after all.'

'It isn't?' asked the girl.

'Every day, it's make your bed, pack your bag and go. That's
about it. Am I right or am I right?'

'Yes, but I thought…'

'And now away with you, niece. I have other things to do
today.'

'But…' her niece protested. 'If I do that… If I go, will I ever
find one?'

'One what?'

'A prince?'

'Ah, probably.' Her aunt drained her tea. 'If you look hard
enough.'

So, the next morning, the girl made her bed, packed her bag,
gave the frog a kiss – which didn't do any good – and left. She
took her golden ball with her.

As she walked, she took a good look around. At the sight
of most of the men, she quickly walked on, but with some of
them she paused to take a closer look. If she liked what she
saw, she pretended to be clumsy and dropped the golden

ball. It bumped onto the ground and rolled away, along the pavement or into the gutter.

She would let out a girlish squeal, put on a sweet and rather helpless expression, and wait to see what happened.

Most of the princes didn't notice the ball, as they were too busy looking at their phones or thinking about themselves. A few bent down and, with a swish of their hair, placed the ball back in the girl's hands.

'You should be more careful, sweetie,' they muttered. 'Looks like an expensive thing.' And then they were gone.

One prince kicked the ball mid-bounce, balanced it on his knee, tapped it from foot to foot a few times before sending it in a neat arc straight into her hand. He looked around as if expecting applause and, when there was none, he ran off in his shiny trainers.

She gave the ball an extra-hard, angry toss when she saw the next prince. It rolled along the pavement, across the road and disappeared into the traffic.

The prince didn't hesitate for a moment but ran after it, slaloming smoothly between cars and buses. What a hero, the girl thought happily, as she stood there, awaiting his return.

But he didn't come back. And neither did her ball.

Disappointed, she sat down on the kerb. No ball, no prince. And it was starting to get late.

'I believe this is yours,' said someone. She looked up and saw a man standing there with her muddy ball in his hand. 'I chased after that scoundrel and dealt with him for you. It's awful that such a thing should happen. Someone stealing from a sweet and beautiful girl like you. Absolutely shocking.'

He polished the ball clean on the bottom of his shirt, which got covered with mud, but what did that matter? He had big brown eyes, beautiful eyelashes, a sweet mouth. And he wasn't green.

The prince helped her to her feet. Her head came up exactly to his shoulder, just as it should.

'A girl with a golden ball…' He had a lovely voice, too. 'It sounds like a fairy tale.'

The café he took her to was filled with the friendly tinkling of cups and spoons. Polite voices spoke quietly, and sweet violin music came through the speakers. The girl and her prince sat with their heads close together, and he clinked his cup against hers.

'What more could a man want?' he said with a smile. 'Good coffee, wonderful company…'

'Tasty biscuit, too,' nibbled the girl.

'Oh, I never eat sugar.' The prince's voice took on a stern edge. 'You shouldn't either, sweetheart.'

'Yes, no, you're right.' The girl quickly put down the rest of the biscuit on her saucer. There was sugar in her coffee, too. She didn't like it without. Luckily, he hadn't noticed that. He was gazing deeply into her eyes.

'Do you know…' he said quietly. 'Actually…'

'Actually what?' the girl purred.

'Actually… I think you should let your hair down. It would really suit you.'

'You think so? I like it up in a ponytail.'

'Oh, no…' The prince ran his fingers through her locks. 'A woman should have long hair. And it should tumble over her shoulders like a waterfall.' Gently, he took out the elastic band.

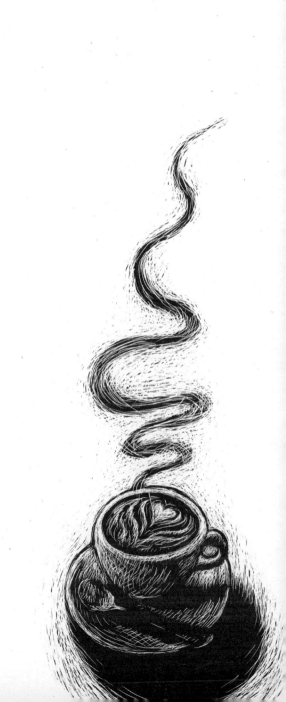

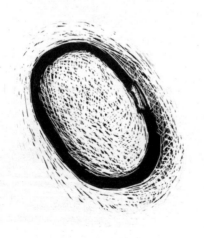

Tangled and knotty, her hair fell down. She quickly combed her fingers through it to tidy it a little.

'I've been out among all those exhaust fumes all day,' she said. 'It's not always like this.'

'A little trim wouldn't hurt,' the prince declared. 'Maybe a bit of a pluck of the old eyebrows? You could be so beautiful if you wanted.'

'Oh,' said the girl. 'Um… thanks.'

'I'll take you to see my hairdresser, okay? And I'll buy you a new dress.'

'What's wrong with this…'

'Nothing. Never mind. Come on, let's not talk about that sort of thing. Don't you agree it was fate that we should meet today? It's like a fairy tale.'

'Life isn't a fairy tale, though,' the girl heard herself say.

'It isn't?' the prince exclaimed.

'Every day, it's make your bed, pack your bag and go. That's what it is.'

'But that's so… prosaic, girl.' The prince pushed his chair back a little. It screeched across the smooth floor.

Oh, she wanted to want him. But she didn't.

No matter how beautiful the prince's eyes were, she missed her frog's faithful gaze. She hadn't even said goodbye to him this morning. Maybe he thought she wasn't coming back. And suddenly that wasn't what she wanted at all.

She picked up her ball and her bag. Came up with a stammered excuse. The prince didn't make much of an effort to stop her.

In the front garden, she could already hear her father laughing, and the frog happily croaking along. Inside, it smelled of toast and chocolate milk and three pairs of eyes looked up at her happily.

'Hello, darling,' her father said. 'You've been out for such a long time.'

'Ah…' she said, putting down her bag under the coatrack. 'It wasn't that long, was it?'

'It did seem long,' said the frog. 'But you're back now.'

Her mother stood up. 'I'll go and start the dinner.'

'Want me to help?'

'No need. You can do the dishes afterwards.'

'Then I'll do the drying.' Her frog jumped onto her arm and snuggled into the crook of her elbow. 'So, how about we give it another try before dinner?' he croaked quietly. 'I have a feeling it might work today. Don't you think?'

The girl looked at his little green body, his wide mouth. No, she didn't think it would work, actually. But she gave him a smile.

'Yes, let's do that,' she said.

BLUE

I

The girls are sitting at the table, each with a book in front of her. Anne has a big thick history book with pages full of little letters, and footnotes at the bottom of the page, which she can barely read and barely understand, but she forces her eyes through the sentences. Next to her, Lisa has a much smaller book, thinner and for younger readers, full of pictures too, which Anne read when she was about five.

Has the Reverend noticed? He doesn't seem to have.

He has barely looked at the sisters, just glanced and nodded when he came in. Now his broad body is sitting in Father's chair, who has had to squeeze himself in beside Mother on the hard bench. All three of them have cups of coffee in front of them and big slices of ginger cake, which Mother has been nervous about all day. She started making it from scratch again twice and still she hardly dared to present it to him, as if it could never be delicious enough for the man with the big beard. The Reverend has not touched the cake yet. He is sitting there and talking, his voice filling the living room. He talks about the council, the news, about the Bible, for a long time. Sometimes Mother and Father say something too, but mostly they just nod.

Anne tries to follow the conversation and to concentrate on her difficult book at the same time. That's already hard enough, but Lisa is constantly fidgeting on the chair beside her. Anne flashes her hateful looks.

'Sit still! Read!'

You're supposed to love your own sister, of course, but Anne does so only very occasionally. The rest of the time she tries to stay as far away from her as possible. It probably doesn't make much difference to Lisa, as everyone else loves her so much. They just do. Without her even trying. It's always been that way, ever since she was a baby beaming away in her cradle. With those little cheeks and eyes and the mouth that was always smiling, even when there was nothing to smile about.

What a little darling, said everyone who came to see her. What a delightful child.

And Anne just stood there beside her.

That was even before Lisa got her long curls, blonder than anyone else's in the whole village, which made everyone stop and watch her as she walked by.

What a treasure. What a beautiful girl.

Beauty is only on the outside, of course, and it's not what matters in this earthly vale of tears, as their parents always told the girls. They had always treated them in exactly the same way and dressed them in the same clothes. Nothing frivolous, nothing special, and Lisa usually got Anne's hand-me-downs. But they didn't look the same on her – oh my goodness, no.

The Reverend has lowered his voice and is leaning in towards her parents.

'There are, um… rumours. I'll admit that. In a village, people gossip. But I assume you pay no heed to such fabrications. Because that's what they are, of course. Lies and fabrications!' he says, raising his voice. Mother and Father are quick to say that they don't listen, that they don't believe that kind of thing, that people who spread such stories belong in hell, even though one should never wish that on anyone, and would the Reverend like another cup of coffee?

The Reverend would indeed. And another piece of ginger cake, as he eats the first one up in two bites. And still chewing, he brings up the subject he actually came here to discuss.

Finally, thinks Anne. Because she's well aware why he's here.

Since the previous girl has gone, he's looking for a new maid. A girl for day and night.

You shouldn't think such things about yourself, of course, but Anne knows she'll be perfect for the job. She is diligent, industrious, clever and modest. And if she wanted to, she could be even better. And she wants that so much!

If I get this chance, she thinks, I'll never do anything bad again. Not commit a single sin, not have any bad thoughts, be good and sweet and patient with everyone. Even with Lisa, which is the hardest thing in the world. But that would be easier then, because they wouldn't see each other during the week, of course.

If she gets the chance. If he picks her. If she goes to live there.

She knows the house. Everyone knows the grand house next to the church with the dark tower. Every Sunday they walk past it in the silent procession.

Anne listens with her entire body, unable to concentrate any longer on the letters in front of her.

To be allowed to be there every day. To be allowed to live there among the books and the sermons. To look after him, to talk to him. To the man who can speak directly to God… How wonderful that would be.

She already knows that she will always agree with him, that she will work hard without complaining or whining, stoking the fire, ironing his clothes, maybe they'll drink tea together in the evening and then she – and she alone – will be allowed to listen to him.

She will never leave him, will defend him against all the nasty gossip going around.

I live with him, she will say. *So, I should know, shouldn't I?* And that will silence all the gossips, until everyone has forgotten all the rumours. She'll make sure of that.

She wants to say all those things to the man with the beard, who is slowly standing up from Father's chair and walking over to the table, but she doesn't say anything, because speaking out of turn is a sin, and no one likes girls who ask questions. So, she says nothing and she asks nothing.

When he comes and stands behind them, she leans more deeply over her difficult book, and the sentences and the dates no longer mean anything, but maybe now he can see what she's reading and he'll be impressed by her intelligence and maybe he'll say something about it, maybe…

The Reverend clears his throat. Anne squeezes her eyes

shut. Please let Mother and Father just say that she can go, without complaining that they can't do without her. They should really consider it an honour that one of their daughters…

'Girls, would one of you…' the Reverend begins. And then he pauses.

Anne slowly opens her eyes and looks to the side. Next to her, she sees that the Reverend has placed his hand, his big hand with the dark hairs on it, on Lisa's shoulder.

'Might you be interested, girl?' he says to Lisa.

II

There are soft mats on the floor. Lisa's footsteps tap across the hard tiles and then disappear when she walks over the carpets. She draws a dotted line of sound throughout the long hallway.

At the end, there is the study where she has to take the coffee at half past seven, half past eight and half past nine precisely. Freshly made every time, and every time with hot milk and three spoonfuls of sugar. If she splashes it into the saucer, the Reverend lifts up the cup and examines the drops dripping from the bottom. And then he looks at her from under his dark eyebrows. He says nothing, just makes an irritated click with his tongue against his teeth.

She has taken to carrying a cloth in her pocket so that, just before she opens the door, after her quiet knock and his quick grunt, she can pat the saucer dry. But the manoeuvre of opening the door with her elbow, carrying in the tray, closing the door again with her back and walking the few steps from door to desk makes the cup tremble on its saucer. Which nearly always sends a little coffee sloshing over the edge.

Again the picking up of the cup, again the look, again the click of the tongue.

'I'm sorry, sir,' she says, but he does not reply and just nods her back out of the room.

She is a disappointment – that much is clear.

Lisa walks back to the kitchen. Along both sides of the hallway, there are doors. She does not yet know what is behind most of them. She doesn't need to know everything, not even what's behind the door upstairs, the one she's not allowed to open. More rooms just mean more work. So much work.

Anne would have been so much better at this, thinks Lisa.

She can picture her walking down the hallway: tray perfectly straight, as if it were weightless (which is not the case – it's made of heavy black wood with metal handles, as if it were made to carry an entire dinner service and not just one cup), knocking the door, carrying it in, putting it down with a smooth movement, and probably managing to say something pleasant or to make a little joke, too. Anne can do that sort of thing. Anne never stands there tongue-tied like Lisa does.

Good morning. Shall I open the window? It's such a beautiful day. Or something along those lines. *I've baked some biscuits. Would you like one?*

Lisa doesn't dare to open any windows or to start baking biscuits. She doesn't dare to do anything that she hasn't expressly been told to do. She's already having to make such an effort not to forget anything.

Fortunately, the Reverend likes her food. He hasn't actually said so, but the plates are always empty when she goes to clear them away. Then, there's more coffee in the study.

It is also fortunate that she no longer has to eat at the table with him, after those first few evenings slowly ticking by, with the sound of the cutlery on the plates and the clock on the wall, as the Reverend chewed and talked, spinning out threads of conversation that Lisa couldn't follow after their first turn.

Anne would be able to. Anne is so clever.

She tried to find a refuge somewhere inside her head and concentrated on clearing her plate. After two bites, her stomach was locked shut.

'That's not healthy for a growing girl,' he had said when she put down her fork. 'Why aren't you eating? Is there something wrong with you?'

She didn't know how to reply and simply picked up her cutlery again.

'A little bit of conversation might be nice now and then, girl,' he said, chewing away.

At home with Mother, Lisa could talk all day long, about this and that and nothing in particular. Now she racked her brain for something nice to talk about but couldn't find anything at all. Only homesickness. And that wasn't allowed, of course, not after you'd been chosen out of all the girls in the village.

'The soup is… um…' was all that she had managed to say in the end. And then she didn't know how to continue.

But he had remained friendly.

'The soup is indeed,' he had said with a smile. And then he'd started talking about St Paul.

How wonderfully Anne would have talked to him. Anne knows about these things.

When she brought the coffee that evening, the cup was in a puddle almost up to its middle.

It's so wrong that she's here, and not her sister. She misses her so much. Most of all when she's lying in bed and there's no other bed to look at, with Anne in it reading a book and angrily turning her back when Lisa asks her to read a story to her.

'Why don't you go and get your own book?'

But Lisa never did that. She preferred to lie watching that angry head of hair, listening to Anne's tossing and turning, to her breathing.

It's so quiet here.

III

It's lovely and quiet here, though, without Lisa's stupid chattering. There's more space in the wardrobe for her dresses, all the drawers are hers now and she never needs to quickly hide anything when her sister comes bursting in. The row of dolls on the shelf above the window is all she left behind – they were too childish to take with her. They stare at Anne, all of them as dumb and empty-headed as Lisa. Lisa who is now *there*.

What is she doing right now? Cooking for him. Sitting with him at the table and talking to him. She has everything. She is allowed to do everything. To clean his shoes, to brush his coat. To know where he is all day, to hear him walking, to be in a room that he might suddenly enter at any moment.

Meanwhile Anne is here, in this house where nothing has changed, with the grey wallpaper, the table, the harmonium, where nothing matters and life consists of waiting until it's Sunday and they can go to church again.

Lisa is allowed to come and join them in their pew. She always grabs her hand and squeezes it and wants to whisper all kinds of things in her ear, but that's not done, of course, not during the service, so Anne pulls her hand away and looks only at the pulpit, at the man standing there with his dark beard and his dark robe, which Lisa has brushed clean that morning.

Then Anne digs her nails into her palms and counts everything down: the singing, the praying, the blessing, until the service is over and she sees her sister walking away with him, across the square to the dark vicarage, a small white figure next to the black robe, glancing back and giving a little wave. Then the two of them go through the gate, and another long and dull week begins.

It's still only Wednesday when the telephone rings. The telephone never rings, it always hangs there, black and silent at the end of the hallway. Father rarely calls anyone, Mother never. Who would they have to call? Everyone they know lives nearby.

Anne didn't even know that the phone made that sound. A fire engine, she thought at first, but when the ringing doesn't stop, she goes into the hallway to take a look. The noise is almost unbearably loud. She lifts the heavy receiver off the hook. The ringing stops.

She holds it up to her ear.

'Anne?' the receiver whispers. 'Anne, could you come over, please?'

'But does the Reverend mind me being here? Have you asked him?'

Lisa shakes her head. 'I didn't dare.'

'Then I'm leaving. I can't be here without his permission. Whatever would he think of me?' But instead of going back out through the door, Anne takes a few more steps into the hallway. The tiles are black and white, the rugs faded red. The doors have large wooden frames. And behind those doors…

'But he'll be back at five, and I need to clean all the floors. All the floors, Anne!' Lisa bites the skin around her thumbnail. 'And if I don't finish it all in time again…'

'Oh, so that's why you asked me to come. I thought you were missing me.'

'I do miss you! I do! You have no idea how much I miss you, Anne!' Her sister tries to give her a hug.

'That's enough of that, you big crybaby.' Anne walks a few more steps along the hallway. She takes in everything around her. The echo of her footsteps. The smell of boiled milk, paper and cigars. She would really like to run her hand over everything. The walls, the coatrack with the heavy black coat hanging from it, the wood of the doors. So many doors.

'There's another hallway like this upstairs,' says Lisa anxiously. 'Even more rooms, and every single one of them has a floor to clean. And an attic. But I don't think that needs cleaning. Will you help me, Anne? Please?'

Anne doesn't reply yet, just walks a few more steps. Halfway down the hallway, there's a wide wooden staircase leading upstairs, and at the end there's a narrower, steeper staircase.

'Have you been in every room of the house?'

Lisa shakes her head. 'I'm not allowed to go everywhere. But I do have these.' She takes a big bunch of keys out of her apron pocket. Keys stick out in every direction, small ones and big ones, rusty ones and shiny ones.

'And what if you don't get it finished this afternoon? What then?' Anne looks at the stairs, at her own feet. Not at her sister.

Lisa gives a big shrug. 'I don't know. Maybe…'

'Will he send you packing?'

'I don't know,' Lisa squeaks.

Anne sees her sister standing in the long hallway. Her curls are escaping from her plait, her apron is far too big and is falling off her shoulders. Anne thinks it would fit her far better – she's nearly a head taller than her sister. Taller than nearly all the boys at school. Stringbean, they always call her. Or worse. Hands too rough, feet too big. But that's good for work. *She* won't need to call her sister for help when she's here. Anne smiles at Lisa.

'Right, let's get started. Where are the buckets?'

IV

It's so nice to have Anne here. Together they carry the buckets. Together they have enough hands to rinse the dirty cloths in the kitchen, with Anne pumping and Lisa wringing. And when they kneel beside each other, scrubbing the tiles, it's as if they're back home, as if everything is good again, and she doesn't have to live here any more. It feels so normal to hear Anne humming out of tune, as she always does when she's working, or to be pushed out of her way: 'Oh, let me do it. It'll be faster!'

Lisa notices that tears keep rolling from the corner of her eye, because it feels so good, and so familiar. If only Anne could stay, if only she didn't have to leave soon, if only they could live here together… But of course that can't happen.

116

Those are stupid thoughts – and her tears are stupid too. She wipes them away and pulls her hair in front of her face, so that her sister won't see them.

The cleaning is not going very quickly, though. Anne seems to be working much more slowly than usual.

'We'll do it thoroughly,' she says, 'or we won't do it at all.' And she's right, of course.

But it's already four o'clock and they've barely finished downstairs. But the steps still need to be done, and upstairs, too. And Anne wants a cup of tea.

'Shouldn't we keep working?'

'I'm tired. I'm thirsty,' Anne gripes. 'I could just go home, you know.'

'Don't go!' trembles Lisa, hurrying to the big kitchen. Anne sits down at the table and looks at her – and how nice it is that her sister can see that she feels so at home here, that she moves so easily, how she picks up the right tin, fills the kettle and waits for the noise of the gas before touching it with a match. And later, too, when Anne wants to see everything and has questions about it all: how the Reverend likes his tea, where the biscuits and the baking trays are and how the catch on the back door works. And Lisa tells her and shows her and Anne really likes her tea, much better than at home, she says, and Lisa is proud and happy – and then suddenly it's half past four.

Lisa hastily bumps upstairs with the buckets, Anne following her a little more slowly with the mop and scrubbing brush. The stairs are soon soaking wet.

'We'll need to dry that too!' Lisa hears herself squeak.

'Calm down,' her sister says. 'We'll get it done.' They start upstairs on the hallway and the first couple of rooms, and time ticks on. They can see the clock on the church tower through the window at the end of the hallway.

'You need to go home soon, Anne. He mustn't see you here. Maybe I should do the rest on my own.'

'No,' says Anne. 'We're in this together.'

She's being so nice today.

They do the master bedroom, Lisa's room, the bathroom, the library and another room full of books – it looks like they're going to manage it all. There are still puddles and wet patches all over the floor. They need mopping up – but then that'll be it. The clock on the tower says it's seven minutes to five. They've made it.

With a sigh of relief, Lisa squeezes the mop into the bucket. Her cheeks are warm and red.

'What about that room?' asks Anne. She points at the door that is still shut. It's a little smaller than the others, and its lock is shiny and new.

Lisa shakes her head. 'I'm not allowed in there.'

'Why not?'

'Don't know.'

'But you do have the key, don't you?'

She shows it to her. It's the smallest key on the bunch. 'But he definitely told me that it's not allowed. Twice, in fact.'

'Well, then you'd better do as he says.'

Lisa nods and picks up the bucket.

'Unless, of course…' her sister says slowly. She has walked over to the door and is looking at the lock. Lisa was about to head downstairs, but she comes back. 'Unless what?'

'Unless he meant something else…'

'Something else? Go, Anne. He mustn't see you here. I don't know what he'll say if…'

'Unless he actually meant that you really should clean that room.'

'Why would he…'

'Maybe he's putting you to the test.'

V

'He's doing what?

'Putting you to the test!' Anne doesn't look at her sister. Outside, on the clock, time ticks on. Seven minutes to five. Six minutes to five. If the Reverend comes home and finds that her sister hasn't finished, or even better, that she's gone into a room where she's not allowed… 'Surely you know what that means, you stupid child?'

'Of course I do.'

'Like in the Bible. When God tells Abraham that he has to sacrifice his son, but He doesn't really mean it. He's just putting him to the test.'

'Oh yes. But…'

'What did the Reverend say?'

'That I'm not allowed to go into that room,' Lisa says nervously.

'No, what did he say before he went out?'

'That I had to do all the floors.'

Anne smiles. 'And "all the floors" means *all* the floors.'

'Do you really think so?' Lisa asks quietly.

Her sister nods.

That's the good thing about being the big sister, Anne thinks. She can always make Lisa do anything she wants. She usually needs to give her just a little push to get her to say yes.

I can have the rest of your pudding, can't I, Lisa?

No, Anne, you've got your own… Oh, please, I'm really… Oh, all right, then.

You dropped that milk bottle, Lisa.

That's not true, Anne! You…

It was you. I saw you do it. It was you. It was you!

And by the third time, Lisa believes it herself. And she confesses and is punished. And Anne is not.

'I'd hurry if I were you.'

'Yes but, yes but, he'll be home any minute and then he'll find me here and…'

'I'll go up into the attic and look out of the window,' Anne offers. 'And I'll shout when I see him coming. And you'll have plenty of time to get it cleaned up.'

'Anne, I really don't think he meant…'

'And I really think he did,' says Anne. 'But please yourself.' She's already taken a few steps towards the attic stairs and smiles when she hears her sister rattling the bunch of keys behind her.

'So… So you'll shout when you see him coming?'

'Oh, I'll shout,' says Anne. 'As soon as I see him.'

Quietly, Anne walks across the large attic to the window at the front. There are so many interesting things up here: books, chairs, dusty boxes and cupboards. But she doesn't look any closer. There'll be time for that. Soon. When this is her attic, her house, her job.

The window at the front is grey with dust. With her sleeve, she wipes a clean circle and looks down. Next to the small front garden is the cemetery with its old and crooked stones; beyond that, the square in front of the church shines in the afternoon sun. It's empty, but someone could come walking across it at any moment.

And she will see him.

But she won't shout.

Lisa always beats her. Always, at everything. And not even because she does her best to win, but just because of how she is. Sweet and pretty and innocent. And nice, so very nice. Everyone always says so. And no matter how hard Anne tries, she can never be as good as her sister. If only because she's so jealous, for envy is, of course, a sin.

But this time is different. This time Lisa's going to get caught.

Ah Lisa, I'm so disappointed in you. Don't you even know how to follow simple instructions? I told you not to go into this room because it's where I keep my... Um... Anne doesn't know exactly what that is. She still needs to imagine what it might be. *My books... the ones that are really difficult, about matters that a highly educated preacher needs to know, but which are completely unsuitable for a girl's eyes. I was trying to protect you, Lisa. And this is how you repay me.*

The Reverend will realise that he made the wrong choice. He will send Lisa home. And then Anne will be allowed to take her place. Finally.

Downstairs, she hears Lisa give a frightened whimper.

Probably because the room is very big or very dirty and she thinks she'll never ever ever get it cleaned in time.

Outside, footsteps slowly approach across the square in front of the church. Calm, purposeful, as only a man can walk.

VI

Let's hope the room isn't too big, thinks Lisa nervously, or too dirty. If she can just clean it in time and lock the room up again in time, then nothing bad is going to happen to her. Is it? If he's not coming home yet, if he's a little delayed… That could happen. It sometimes does. Has the bell already rung five? She didn't hear it.

'Anne? Do you see anyone coming?'

'No,' Anne calls down. 'There's no one out there. Plenty of time.'

Lisa puts the key in the lock. It turns very easily. She picks up the heavy bucket and pushes the door open.

Her first thought is that she'll never get this room clean. Not with what's hanging up there and lying over there and – oh, look at the state of the floor!

Her second thought is that she would be much better off not seeing what she's seeing.

She wants to slam the door shut, but her hand has let go of the bucket, which clatters onto its side, as buckets normally do, and the water splashes out, as water normally does. She feels her stockings and shoes getting wet – and all of that feels very normal too.

But what she sees is not normal at all.

The girls have their eyes open and are staring at her, like her dolls at home on the shelf. There are faces she knows, girls she's heard stories about, about their sad and worried and angry parents, girls who have been prayed for: that they might soon return to the safety of the flock. Who have been gossiped about in the village. Who have obviously snuck off, in pursuit of their own pleasure. Sinful, ungrateful, unreliable girls.

None of that is true.

Lisa stumbles backwards, trips over the bucket, lands in the puddle. And then she thinks only one thing.

'Anne!' she screams. 'Anne go away go home leave now Anne. Now!'

Her sister seems to be listening to her for once: she hears Anne's feet hurrying down the attic stairs. The pantry door closes as the front door opens.

She hears footsteps coming into the house.

She hears footsteps climbing the stairs.

She tries to close the door, but her hands are shaking and the bucket is in the way, so she kicks it aside, but that makes such a clattering racket and everything is still lying there on the floor: the mop, the bucket, the water – and what's that in the water? Is it blood?

'Lisa, are you upstairs?' the Reverend shouts. 'These stairs are sopping wet. Blast it all!'

Lisa stands in the middle of the hallway, as if she's on a railway track with a train thundering along it towards her.

Thank goodness Anne has left, is all she thinks. Thank goodness Anne's gone home.

But Anne has not gone home. That's the last thing on her mind.

In deadly silence, she climbs the back stairs, one step at a time, then tiptoes along until she is standing just around the corner from the hallway. Which is how she hears everything that is said.

'Lisa Lisa Lisa…' she hears the Reverend's voice. 'So, you've gone and done it after all. And I thought I could trust you.' He laughs a little strangely. He does not sound happy. 'I didn't actually think you'd have the courage to go into that room. Such a timid little mouse.'

Anne hears her sister sobbing quietly. This is going well.

'What is it with you women? Why can't you just leave things well alone? Eve and the apple, Pandora and the box. You simply can't resist, can you?'

I'll just sneak downstairs now, thinks Anne. Then go home and wait to see what happens. For Lisa to get sent home: fired, shamefully dismissed. And then – hopefully – for the Reverend himself to come round and say that sadly he made the wrong choice. And that he'd like to correct his mistake if possible, by picking the right sister this time.

'And what's it brought you? Nothing but misery. You have only yourself to blame, Lisa. For everything that's about to happen.'

Exactly, thinks Anne. She creeps through the pantry to the back door. No matter what Lisa might claim, Anne has never been here. She hasn't broken any rules, she didn't go into the forbidden room, not her. From now on, she will only be obedient and well behaved for the rest of her life.

She's already holding the door handle when she hears her sister scream.

Anne freezes. For a moment she doesn't know what to do. This wasn't part of her plan. What a drama queen, she thinks, but when Lisa screams again and then suddenly stops, she doesn't think that any more.

Her head is empty, and her body is just standing there.

Suddenly she sees herself long ago, when she was only five or so, but she already had to spend all afternoon taking care of Lisa, who would look through the bars of her cot and smile at her big sister, with those little cheeks and those little eyes and those sweet little lips, and then later she would pull her by the hand all around the village and sing endless songs about how Little Lisa loves living on Lime Tree Lane – and suddenly Anne stops thinking her Anne thoughts, stops being sensible and obedient and well behaved, and instead spins around and runs back up there, back upstairs.

Halfway along the corridor, a dark figure is holding her sister. By her throat, it seems, but that's not possible, that could never happen, but she sees it anyway, and she sees her sister writhing and fighting, but she's clearly no match for the big man in the black coat, and Anne who is no longer Anne lets out a huge roar and, lowering her head, charges at the two of them.

It is the shock that makes the Reverend lose his balance. And, of course, the puddles of water at the top of the stairs.

As he falls, he looks in amazement from the one sister to the other, from the pretty one to the ugly one, and he lets go of the pretty one, and the ugly one lashes out with her foot – and it's just a girl, of course, and for a brief second he looks surprised that such a thing can kick so hard, but then his own feet are treading on thin air, his hands are trying to grasp the banister but gravity gets the better of him – and there he goes. Bumping and cracking, his head hits each of the stairs, one after the other. One last bump, and then silence.

Now it's Anne who starts crying. Lisa stands up and takes her by the hand.

Step by step, they climb down the stairs. Slowly at first, because they don't want to look at what's lying down there, and then very quickly, because they need to pass close by it, and what if a hand were to suddenly reach out and grab an ankle? But that does not happen. Nothing is moving here but the two girls.

They run, their feet slapping through the long hallway to the front door. Only Anne looks back for a moment.

The man in the dark coat is still lying there, half on the bottom step. In the shadow of the stairs, she can just make out his face, a patch of white against his beard, which is so black. So black that it's almost blue.

SLEEPER

I

The girls were born on the same day, to the same mother. But they were not much alike.

One of the girls was a little sweeter and a little prettier. She sang just that little bit better, got better marks at school. And there was something else about her.

'As far as I can see, there's little to be done,' said the doctor. 'Actually, more or less absolutely nothing. I'm terribly sorry.' Like some kind of wicked fairy issuing a curse, he drew a cross on the calendar. 'She has until then. I could be a couple of months out, but no more than that, I'm afraid.'

He said it quietly, but it was as if he'd shouted it across the small room. That was how shocked they were: the father, the mother and the two sisters.

The mother and the sisters started crying; the father clenched his fists as if he wanted to hit someone. When the doctor cowered behind his desk, the father hit his desk instead.

'No!' he shouted. 'No, I won't stand for it! That is not going to happen. No!'

As soon as he got home, he started writing to other doctors, near and far. He paid well, so they all came and examined the girl, who now spent most of her time in bed. They prodded her, poked her, stuck needles into her, looked as deep inside her as they could, but when they were done, they all said the same thing.

'Not much longer. Months. Maybe weeks.'

'That's impossible!' Father yelled. 'There must be some better doctors out there! Better than this bunch of quacks!'

'Shall I ask my sister?' said Mother. 'Maybe she knows what to do.'

'That old witch?' Father shrieked. 'What could she do to help?'

He could no longer sit, or stand, or sleep. He searched for doctors, more and more outlandish ones, from further and further away, wearing masks on their faces and clothed in strange garb. The fees they charged also grew higher and higher. They sang strange songs to the girl, gave her horrible potions, burned pieces of wood, performed dances beside her bed. But after they had done everything they could, they shook their heads, too.

'Not much longer. Weeks. Maybe days.'

'Then stop time!' Father yelled. 'Smash the clocks, burn the calendars!'

He made a big fire in the garden and threw time onto it. Calendars, hourglasses, watches, the newspaper that came every day.

'Where there's no time, time cannot pass!' he cried.

The neighbours closed their windows to keep out the smoke. They sat indoors, sighing deeply. In sympathy, but also because they knew that life didn't work that way. Maybe Father knew that himself as well, because he went on looking, every day, for different doctors who would say something new. Every evening he was more tired when he came home.

'Any change?' he asked, the moment he came through the door.

The girls' mother shook her head and said nothing.

Father put the sick girl on his lap and stroked her, buried his face in her hair, kissed her as if he wanted to drink her all up.

'You're still here,' he said. 'You're still here.'

Quieter and quieter, the girl hung in his arms.

In the corner, the girl's sister sat and watched everything that happened. She could feel time ticking away inside her too, all the hours she had left with her sister. There was still so much she wanted to do with her: skipping, playing snakes and ladders, making up funny stories. But there was no time for anything now, her sister was too tired and they were never alone, just the two of them.

She looked at her sad parents, who hardly ever looked back at her.

They're not saying it, she thought, but of course they're thinking it. Everyone's thinking it: why isn't it the other one? Her sister was prettier and sweeter and good at school, while she just sat there daydreaming in the classroom. She only had to pick up a pen and it started leaking. If she cooked something, people ate it out of politeness. Her parents would be much less sad if she was the one who was going to die.

She wished she could change that. But she had no idea how.

Father had tried everything by now, and nothing had helped. The sick girl became more and more tired and quiet until eventually all she did was sleep. Her father sat beside the bed, leafing through his papers and leaflets with increasing desperation. There were no doctors left to call.

'I've asked my sister to come round this evening,' said Mother.

'Really? Why? Surely you don't think there's anything she can do?'

'I don't think anything at all. I'd just like to see her.'

'As long as it's not too tiring,' growled Father. 'All the time my little girl has left is for me!'

That evening, the girls' aunt came tiptoeing into the bedroom. Downstairs in the halfway she had hugged her sister for what must have been a quarter of an hour before they were able to say anything to each other. Now she looked at her niece in bed for a moment before walking over to her other niece, who was sitting quietly on a chair. She gave her a kiss, a wink, and also a present – for her birthday, she said. It was a skipping rope.

The girl turned the rope and did a little skip.

'No noise!' Father hissed immediately. He glared at his sister-in-law. 'Ugh, if that's all you've brought, then you might as well just leave.'

Auntie gave her startled niece a kiss and gently guided her out of the room.

'Why don't you go and skip in the garden?'

When the girl had left, she took a closer look at the girl in bed. She laid one hand on the pale forehead.

'Not much longer now,' she said quietly to her brother-in-law.

'Tell me something I don't know.'

'Well, I'll tell you this right now: I can't cure her.'

'In that case, you'd better just clear off.'

'But there is something else I can do.' Auntie took a small bottle from her handbag, with a little silver spoon. 'This will make her sleep peacefully.'

'She's already sleeping very peacefully,' said Father, his rage barely concealed. 'That is not the point.'

'I know that. But this will ensure that she goes on sleeping.'

'What do you mean?' Mother had just come in with coffee. 'Do you mean…'

'Yes, that's what I mean. She'll go on sleeping. She won't die.'

'She won't?'

'No. She'll sleep until… Until it's time to wake up.'

'Oh yes, of course,' grumbled Father. 'Until a prince comes and kisses her awake, no doubt.'

'Maybe. It does happen. Or maybe not. Maybe it'll take a very long time. But she'll be breathing. She'll be alive.'

'Alive…' A tiny spark of hope came into Father's eyes. He looked at his daughter in the bed. He would do anything for her. Anything.

His sister-in-law dripped a couple of drops onto the spoon and held it up to the girl's lips. She swallowed obediently and gave a small sigh.

You had to look very closely to see the change, but it was there. Her breath became a little deeper, her cheeks a little less pale.

'A couple of drops every week,' said Auntie. 'That's all.'

'That's all?' Father thought angrily about the pills and potions he'd spent all his money on. He couldn't bring himself to say, 'Thank you', but he slowly nodded at his sister-in-law.

'But how long will it be?' asked Mother. 'Before a prince comes along?'

'I don't know.'

'Isn't there anything at all that you can tell us?'

Auntie shook her head.

'Oh, but maybe there is,' she said slowly. 'There is one thing.'

'Yes? What?'

'The two of you have another daughter.'

For a moment, the two parents had felt a little hopeful, but now they sank back into their chairs.

'Oh yes,' they muttered.

They could hear her skipping, outside on the grass. She was counting as she skipped, from one to a hundred and back again.

II

The girl slept, gently breathing the sheet up and down.

Her parents had carried everything upstairs: the chairs and the coffee table, the reading lamp, the basket of knitting and crossword puzzles. The bedroom had turned into a living room. The cat was asleep on the foot of the bed. Mother and Father pulled their chairs up close, one on either side, each holding a little white hand in their own. They watched for every quiver of her eyelashes, listened for every little sigh.

'She's asleep,' they said to each other. 'She's breathing. She's still here.'

It was the other girl who still went up and down the stairs, did the cooking and went shopping. The front door was more and more difficult for her to open every time, as the weeds and bushes around the house had grown so high. The roses, in particular, with their twisting branches and their cruel thorns, grew all over everything. At first, the girl cut them back, but they grew again, thicker and tougher. Luckily, she was becoming thinner and thinner, so the door only needed to open very slightly. The garden shears lay rusting on the mat.

As the seasons passed, the roses grew higher and higher, reaching all the way up to the bedroom window. In the summer, they bloomed beautifully, until their petals withered and fell, and winter came once more.

The girl slept.

Her sister made lots of apple sauce from the fruit in the back garden and cooked pancakes to go with it, which didn't require many ingredients. The girls' parents didn't eat much anyway. They usually slept in their chairs, waking up only to look at their daughter in bed.

'Is she still breathing?' they would ask.

And the sister nodded. 'She's still breathing. Go back to sleep.'

So, they went back to sleep. They grew older, thinner and more desperate.

No prince came.

III

It was spring again. How many springs had come and gone?

A hundred years had passed. At least that was how it seemed to the girl.

Down in the cellar lay her parents, washed and embalmed. They had both died with her sister's name on their lips. They had both made her promise that she would stay – stay and watch, stay and wait.

'Of course,' she had said. 'Of course, I'll stay.' And stay she did.

No prince had come. And everything was gone. She could no longer open the door. The house had become a tomb.

The cat was dead too, or had run away.

When she looked in the mirror, she no longer recognised herself.

Still, her sister lay safely beneath the sheets. She washed them every week, taking care not to disturb her. Then she gave her the drops from her aunt; there was only a small amount left in the bottle. She sat on the edge of the bed, looking at her sister lying there with her eyes closed.

'What did your eyes look like again?' she whispered. 'I can't remember. Or what your voice sounded like. I've forgotten everything.' She sighed. How many days was it since she'd eaten the last scrap of pancake made from the very last scoop of flour? She didn't remember that either. But she wasn't hungry.

'Maybe I'm dead too,' she said.

But she wasn't, because she could hear something, down below in the garden.

It was the sound of cracking and tugging. The rosebushes outside the window swished to and fro, and someone out there was cursing and panting.

It felt as if she needed to wake up first – and only then could she understand what she was hearing. A wild boar perhaps? A stray dog? She'd given up hoping for a prince long ago. But it was indeed a prince – she could see his elegant plumed hat moving out there among the roses.

'Sister,' she said. 'He's here.' She slowly got to her feet, legs shaking with hunger and from not moving for such a long time.

'And in the nick of time,' she said, smiling at the girl in the bed. 'I'll go and fetch him for you. Don't go anywhere!'

She put on her mother's old dressing-gown – her own clothes had all become too small – tied it tightly and stumbled downstairs.

From outside, she heard more tugging and sawing and quite a few 'ow!'s, too. On the doormat, she found the rusty shears. She pulled the front door as hard as she could. The roses had wrapped themselves around the doorknob and were growing in through the letterbox. With the blunt shears, she cut away as much as she could. The thorns hooked into her fingers. They bled, but she kept pulling and finally she managed to open the door, just a very small crack.

'Over here, Your Highness!' she called. 'Keep it up! I'll meet you halfway, too!'

The two of them cut through the roses, fighting a slow path towards each other. Puffing and panting, clothes torn to shreds, covered in blood and scratches, they finally stood face to face on the mat.

Was he really a prince? He was bleeding and exhausted and had rose petals in his hair. But what did it matter?

'At last,' said the girl. 'Come on. Upstairs.' She took his hand and pulled him along the hallway, which stank and was full of bin bags, up the stairs littered with dirty dishes and old

clothes, and towards the bedroom. He glanced at the mess but didn't mention it. Which was nice of him.

Upstairs, it was even filthier. She hadn't opened a window for months, hadn't even washed herself. Whatever must he think?

'Sorry about all this,' she said. 'But she's been washed, and the sheets have just been changed.'

She led him to the bedroom door, opened it, and was about to pull her hand away from his and step back.

So, this is it, she thought. Done.

She suddenly felt how hungry she was, how stiff and sore and dirty, and realised how much she wanted a hot bath and then something to eat. Maybe she could start with…

He did not let go of her hand.

He also wasn't looking in the right direction, wasn't walking to the bed to kneel beside her sister.

'Well, what are you waiting for?' she said angrily. 'Go on! Kiss!'

He turned around and kissed. But not the right mouth.

She spluttered and spat him away.

'No, you fool. Not me! You're here for her! You're supposed to kiss her awake!'

'Her?' The prince looked at the bed. 'Absolutely not. She's far too young. And, um…'

'And what?'

'I think she's, er, dead. And has been for some time.'

The girl looked at her sister in the bed. She could see it now. How had she not noticed before? She walked over to her, took her hand. It was so small, and as cold as a stone.

'She's dead…' she whispered.

'I'm sorry,' the prince said with a sympathetic nod. 'But you're not,' he added cheerfully.

'I'm not?'

The girl looked around at the grey and dirty room. It was dark, as the roses at the window let in barely any light. But through the branches, she could make out small patches of sky. It was blue – and it was brilliant.

'No,' she said slowly. 'No, I don't think I am.'

MONSTER GIRL

Storm

The girl is embroidering in the turret room. With small cross-stitches, she is working on the final letter, the E at the end: PATIENCE IS A VIRTUE.

Princesses are supposed to be able to embroider beautifully, but her work never really turns out well. Her fingers are too large and clumsy for the little needle. She pricks herself, the thread becomes tangled, and her stitches are neither small nor neat enough, according to the good lady Morsegat. The lady is sitting at her desk, reading a useful book, and yet still she always sees everything the girl does.

'Eyes on your work, princess,' she says whenever the girl wants to look out of the window.

Today, the girl's eyes will not stop wandering. The wind is blowing outside, and the windows are rattling restlessly. The sky in the distance is dark, and the sea below is wide and empty all the way to the horizon.

The girl knows that, one day, a prince will come sailing across that sea. A prince who has come from afar to find her.

His sail will be as white as his teeth, and she will be allowed to go with him. His realm lies over the ocean, blue his eyes, blue his blood. And then he sees her, and then he kisses her. And then, and then…

And then they will both live happily ever after. But not yet, of course. She is not ready to face a prince, nowhere near, nowhere near. He would have the fright of his life.

She embroiders the last cross of the E and sighs as she looks at all the letters she still needs to decorate with little hearts and flowers: the P, the Ts and the A, and the V, and the Es and… She has more tasks than there are clouds above the sea.

The wind blows along even more clouds to join them, thunder-headed and grey. Lightning flashes in the distance, and the rain lashes against the windows. Eyes on your work, princess, she says to herself. And then she sees something.

Far, far away, caught in a ray of sunshine that is peeping through the clouds, a small white triangle is gleaming. It flaps and flutters and tumbles in the wind.

She suddenly feels very nervous. Could it be him? Now? Today? She puts down her needle.

'**LOOK**,' she points. '**THERE!**'

The good lady Morsegat does not so much as glance up from her book.

'Don't shriek like that. A princess speaks quietly, princess.'

'**BUT I CAN SEE SOMETHING!**' The girl stands up, PATIENCE IS A VIRTUE slipping from her lap and onto the floor. '**THERE'S SOMETHING SAILING OUT THERE!**' She speaks as quietly as she can, and yet her voice fills the small room. '**A SHIP!**'

'A ship? Of course not. It's just your imagination, princess.'

Of course, it's just her imagination.

Back when she first came to live here, she used to see a ship in every foaming crest. Her heart leaping, she would dash to the window every time. Here he comes, she thought. At last. And she felt happy and scared, both at the same time.

But it was always something else: a wave, some splashing foam, the smooth back of a whale. Or, once a month, the supply boat. Never a ship, never a prince.

'On your chair, princess. And pick your work up off the floor. We don't want it to get dusty.'

Obediently, the girl sits down, but her eyes keep looking at the window. It is raining harder now, the drops drawing lines down the glass. As she peers through them, the ship seems to appear and then disappear over and over again. It battles against the storm. She sees the sail tearing, the mast snapping like a dry branch. Then a wave takes everything – and the sea is empty once more.

If it was her prince, then he is now a drowned prince.

'Oh no, princess…' The good lady Morsegat has come to stand beside the princess's desk and is shaking her head as she looks at her embroidery. 'That final E is far too clumsy. It looks like a B! VIRTUB! That's what it says. I have no idea what a virtub might be, but it clearly has nothing to do with patience. Unpick the stitches and start over.'

The girl picks up her needle again. The wind takes another deep breath and blows around the tower.

'Brr,' shivers the good lady Morsegat. 'What beastly weather! We shall have to postpone our evening walk for today.'

Drowning

They take their walk the next morning instead. Skipping a walk is not permitted, because walking is good for the muscles and the circulation, and having a breath of fresh air every day is essential for a princess. They walk down the path past the tower to the little beach. There is not much more walking to be done on such a small island.

The girl is a good two feet taller than her companion, so she spots it first. There is something lying near the tideline: a bulky shape, still half in the water.

'Oh, ugh, a dead seal,' says the good lady Morsegat with a sigh. 'I do hope it's not going to smell.'

But it is not a seal, as they see when they come closer. Arms and legs wide outspread, a man is lying on the beach. His shirt, grey with dirt and green with seaweed, is clinging to his back. One of the sleeves is dark red.

With three big steps, the girl is beside him. Her feet sink deep into the sand. The hollows they leave quickly fill with seawater.

'Princess! No! Don't touch it!' The good lady Morsegat chooses to stay on the path. 'Leave it there, the sea will carry it away.'

The girl stands beside the motionless body. No, it is not a prince. His hair is stubbly, a ring gleams in his ear, and what she can see of his brown arms is covered in wild tattoos. *Thief of Hearts*, she reads. *Stormcurse*. The left arm is at a strange angle.

'Come along, princess. The sea is cruel. That's just how it is. Let it be a lesson to you.' The good lady Morsegat turns around and starts to head back. 'Come along, it's time for your geography lesson.'

'BUT HE'S BREATHING,' says the girl. The man's chest is going up and down, and a groaning sound is coming from his mouth. 'HE'S STILL ALIVE!'

'Oh, heavens! Really?' The good lady Morsegat does not wish to get sand on her skirts, so she lifts them high as she approaches with dainty little steps. 'Don't touch it, princess.'

But the girl has already leaned over the man and taken him by the shoulders and is dragging him higher up onto the sand. Her arms are so strong that it is easy for her. Gently, she turns him onto his back. His throat and cheeks are all stubble and grains of sand. Moaning, he gropes at his blood-soaked sleeve with his good hand.

'Didn't you hear me? This is none of our business. Come on, we're going inside now.'

The girl always does as the good lady Morsegat says, but this time it is as if she does not hear her. She takes off her pink waistcoat and lays it carefully under the bruised head. It is a nasty, itchy piece of clothing, but it must surely be softer to lie on than the hard sand. The cool wind blows under her shirt.

'For heaven's sake, keep your clothes on!' the good lady gasps. 'A princess must dress decently at all times!'

Inside the pocket of her skirt, the girl finds the sampler she was working on yesterday, PATIENCE IS A VIRTUB. She uses it to gently dab away some of the blood. The head on the pink waistcoat blinks its eyes.

'Leave it!' The good lady Morsegat pushes her hand away. 'You're only making things worse. First aid is one of my professional responsibilities, so I know exactly what…'

The eyes open, big and brown. They look the girl straight in the face.

'HELLO, SIR,' she says shyly. 'ARE YOU ALL RIGHT? DOES YOUR ARM HURT?' Maybe she can pick him up and carry him to the tower, maybe she can…

'Wraaawh!' With a hoarse cry, the shipwrecked man claws his way through the sand, away from her. 'Blimey! You nearly gave me a heart attack!'

His shock shocks her, too. It's her fault, of course. Because she's a monster. Ugly and terrifying.

She stands up, stumbles backwards and runs to the tower. Bonk bonk, go her feet.

'Hey!' he shouts after her. 'What… Where… Wait a second!'

She does not wait. Two steps at a time, she climbs the stairs and slams the door behind her.

Up in the tower, she stands in front of the mirror.

Monster – that is what she sees. A monster's nose, a monster's chin. Beneath that, a monster's body, like some vast thing wrapped around her. Which is always bumping into things and knocking them over. Which only fits into dresses and corsets when she sucks her breath in deep. With nails like claws, no matter how often she files them. And oh, all that hair all over everywhere she can see. And it's probably even worse on her back.

She is terrible. She is not fit to be seen.

For a time, she had forgotten, but now she remembers.

153

After a while, she dares to look through the window again, peeking from behind the curtain. Down below, the man has stood up and is shakily limping towards the storage shed with the good lady Morsegat. When he looks up, she dives behind the curtain.

Baby

Of course, her poor parents had also got the shock of their lives.

The newborn princess did not fit into any of the little lace gowns that were waiting for her or into any crib. She had to be hauled away by two of the servants, who deposited her in one of the guest beds. After all, there would be no guests.

'We can never receive guests again!' wailed the queen. 'Not with *that* in the house. The shame would kill me!'

She and the king stood and stared at the sleeping lump under the tiny sheet. Where had it come from? How did it turn out like that? they wondered. We're completely normal, aren't we?

They looked at each other again, just to make sure.

No, not too big, not too small, and certainly not hairy or behorned or in any way strange.

'And then we produce something like that,' sobbed the queen. 'A... A...'

She did not say 'monster'. But they were both thinking it.

'Oh well, I'm sure it's not that bad,' the king said optimistically. 'If you look... kind of through your eyelashes, then it seems like... She's not so... And maybe it'll all turn out fine? Maybe she'll... grow out of it?'

'Of course it's not going to turn out fine!' The queen was inconsolable.

The curtains were closed, and the christening party was cancelled.

'No one gets to see her,' the queen sniffed. 'No one!'

Breakfast

'No one?' The sailor looks out over the water. 'No one else washed ashore? I'm the only one?'

His arm is hanging in the sling that the good lady Morsegat has skilfully made for him. The wound is a bad one, and he cannot put his weight on his ankle yet. He slept on a flour sack in the shed, a whole day and a whole night, and now he is standing on their little beach, limping and cursing.

The girl slowly approaches along the path. Her knees bent a little, so as to look smaller, her corset pulled tight. She would rather not have come outside, but rules are rules, and the morning walk is part of the routine.

'We cannot shirk our duties simply because we have an uninvited guest, princess.'

Fortunately, the uninvited guest is not looking at the girl. He is staring at the water, as if expecting someone else to emerge from the waves. Which, of course, does not happen.

'I'm sorry,' says the good lady Morsegat. 'You were the only one we found.'

'Hell, thunder and the pox!'

'Could you perhaps express yourself in a more seemly manner? That's no language for the ears of a young, impressionable girl.'

The sailor does not appear to hear her. He kicks the water, as if he wants to hurt the sea, and then his ankle gives way and he falls to his knees in the surf.

'Ow! God's teeth and testicles!' He curses again and spits out a mouthful of water. 'Bill! You pillock! You idiot! You should have steadied the helm!'

'Come back inside, princess. This is not going to prove instructive in any way.'

The beach is covered with smooth grey stones. The sailor picks up a handful and throws them after the sunken ship. 'Stew! Nelius! You stupid idiots! Leaving me here on my own!'

'Compassion is called for here, princess,' the good lady Morsegat instructs her, turning to walk away. She pauses to address the sailor: 'We are sincerely sorry for the loss of your companions.'

'Loss? They're no great loss!' The sailor tosses one stone after another. 'They were idiots! Complete muttonheads! Each and every one!'

'If you feel able to climb the steps, breakfast will be served up at the tower.'

'I'm glad they drowned!' he yells, but the girl sees that he is wiping his eyes and blowing his nose on something white that can only be her badly embroidered sampler.

He coughs a few times and spits into the water.

Then he decides that he wants breakfast.

At the table, the sailor does everything the girl has been taught not to do: gobbling, slurping, helping himself without being invited to. The good lady Morsegat can hardly say anything about it, as he is not her charge. The glares she flashes at him would make the girl cringe, but the sailor just goes on eating.

Princess

She tries not to look at him too often and to keep her eyes on her own plate. Princesses eat only tiny morsels. Lettuce leaves. Slices of tomato. Once a week, a soft-boiled egg. She is always hungry. And yet still she is far too heavy and she has to hold her breath harder and harder every day to do up her corset. But breathing is less important than a pretty waist, and a princess's waist should be as thin as a wasp's.

The sailor polishes off the entire month's supply of eggs and wipes his mouth on the tablecloth. Then he finally looks up from his plate.

'What is this place?' he says. 'What are you two doing here, in the middle of…' He stares out of the window. 'In the middle of absolutely nowhere?' He struggles to his feet and limps around the small turret room, past desks and lecterns, past the storage cupboard, the walls with their shelves full of prints, sewing baskets, educational books:

Everything a Young Lady is Required and Permitted to Know
Physical Exercises and Dietary Advice
The Seven Virtues and Their Applications

'Seven virtues,' he mumbles. 'Blimey. The seven seas, that's what I know. The Dead Sea, the Red Sea, the Great Sea, the Still Sea…'

'How interesting.' The good lady Morsegat starts stacking the plates. 'Maybe during our geography lesson you could show us on the map which places you've visited.'

'Of course. I've been all over.' He looks at the girl, who is staring at her plate. 'And I thought I'd seen everything…'

'But not right now, unfortunately. As always, we have a busy programme.'

'You do?' says the sailor.

'Absolutely. A princess requires a thorough education, and that's no small matter.'

'It isn't?'

'Heavens, no. She still has so much to learn before she is ready for the big day. And it's not going too smoothly.'

'Oh,' says the sailor. Across the table, two pairs of eyes look at the monster girl sitting on her chair, which is too small for her. Her knees only just fit under the table.

'But we shall not despair. Patience is a virtue. Isn't that right, princess?'

The girl pushes back her chair, stands up and leaves the room.

'Princess!' the good lady Morsegat calls after her. 'When we leave the table, we say, "Many thanks, I have had a sufficiency."'

But the girl has already slammed her bedroom door.

Behind her, she hears the sailor say, 'I'd like more… um, of a sufficiency. Awright?'

Potions

Oh, the princess certainly grew, but she did not grow out of it. When she played, the mirrors in the empty corridors trembled. When she cried, the whole palace shook. And she cried a lot. It gave the queen migraines.

'Then go and comfort her!' her husband said.

The queen shrugged. 'What am I supposed to say?'

'You know,' said the king. 'Nice things. Kind things.'

But nice, kind things never came into the queen's mind when she saw her daughter. So hairy, so toothy, so terribly big… She had wanted to have a daughter she could dress

prettily, to show her off on jaunts around the city. And she wanted to throw parties again and to receive guests. But none of that was possible with *that* in the house.

And none of the doctors knew what to do.

Shrinking potions, therapeutic baths, diets of sour milk…

Nothing helped. Nothing changed the princess's appearance.

'Well, sometimes these things just happen, Sire,' the doctors said. They had to shout a little to make themselves heard above the noise in the nursery. 'I'm afraid you'll have to learn to live with it.'

'What good are you to me?' shouted the king. 'Get lost, the lot of you!'

And get lost they did, as quickly and as politely as they could.

Holding his unshaven cheeks in his hands, the king sat on his throne. Howling came from his daughter's room, and sobbing from his wife's boudoir. How was he supposed to concentrate on ruling the country? Because he also had a job to do, of course.

Bother, he thought angrily. Bother and fuss. This has to end – and soon.

Chest

The sailor brings bother and fuss. He scuttles across the beach down below, drags wreckage from the surf and shouts a bit at the seagulls, who yell back at him just as loudly. The girl keeps looking outside. She is supposed to be studying her history lesson, she is terribly behind with her times tables, and where on earth is her embroidery?

'I DON'T KNOW,' she whispers. 'LOST IT OR SOMETHING. I'M SORRY.'

But she knows very well where it is: covered in snot and stuffed into a trouser pocket down on the beach.

'It was most careless of you to treat your work like that. A princess is always proper and precise.' The good lady Morsegat takes a clean piece of white cloth from the cupboard. 'But I shall turn a blind eye on this occasion. Start over.'

One by one, she will have to trace out the letters and then fill them in, one cross-stitch at a time. The P and the A and the T…

'And work more neatly this time. Not too hastily. Patience is, after all, a virtue.'

Down below, the sailor is dragging empty barrels out of the waves. He turns them upside down and sits, with his head in his hands, staring at the horizon. There is not much to see. The sea is empty, as empty as the princess's new embroidery cloth.

'Eyes on your work, princess,' says the good lady Morsegat.

'There,' says the sailor, pointing, as the two ladies walk past that evening. 'That's one of ours!'

Just off the coast, a wooden chest is bobbing in the waves. The sea keeps pushing it a little closer and then pulling it back. Almost as if it's teasing him.

On one good leg and one bad leg, the sailor limps through the surf. He has found a long, fraying rope, which he is trying to throw around the chest like a lasso. It's not easy with one arm. A couple of times, he nearly does it, but the rope keeps slipping into the water. The waves toss the chest back and forth, back and forth, back and forth. *Haha*, they say. *Don't think so.*

'I wouldn't put too much weight on your leg,' says the good lady Morsegat. 'That won't help the healing process.'

'Probably not,' growls the sailor. 'But I want that chest.'

'We can't always get what we want. That's the lesson to be learned here.'

'Hey, lady,' snorts the sailor, 'maybe that stuff works with her, but not with me. I want my goddamned chest.'

'If you use such blasphemous language, we shall stop talking to you. Cover your ears, princess. It's time for tea and your dictation.'

Obediently, the girl claps her hands over her ears, but not so tightly that she can no longer hear the cursing. These words are new to her. They land somewhere inside her like the seeds of an exotic plant. Dirty rotten. Hell's thunder. Goddamned chest.

The good lady Morsegat has quickly walked on, but the girl stands and watches as the sailor throws the rope again. It splashes into the water. Another miss.

'Hey, are you laughing at me?'

The girl gasps and shakes her head. Of course not. She just wanted to see if he would manage to haul it in, that goddamned chest. What would it feel like to say that word out loud?

'Hey, girl, could you just get it out of the water for me? What do you say?'

She is startled. Her?

'I'd do it myself, but um…' He holds out his ankle.

'**PRINCESSES DON'T SWIM**,' she mumbles.

'You don't have to swim. It's not that deep. And you're more than tall enough, eh?'

Her cheeks flush. Far too tall, far too big, far too…

'A few steps and you'll have it. Go on, sweetheart…'

The girl hesitates. The water is strictly forbidden. Getting wet is also strictly forbidden. But on the other hand, princesses are supposed to help their fellow human beings. DO AS YOU WOULD BE DONE BY, as she embroidered only recently.

'Go on, lass. Do it for me.'

She looks around. The good lady Morsegat is not there to say no. The sailor gives her a big grin and she smiles a half-smile back at him.

Maybe she can just dash in there and grab it, that dirty rotten goddamned chest.

And before she realises what she's doing, she has kicked off her shoes, which as always are too small (princesses have such sweet little feet), and taken a few steps into the water. The waves wash around her calves. The sand is soft, and the sea is wonderfully cold on her toes.

'Princess!' calls a voice from the shore. 'What on earth are you doing? You're not going swimming, are you?!'

She does not need to swim. She is still sticking out far above the waves as she takes a few more steps through the surf. The sea tugs at her skirts, making them heavy. But she feels wonderfully lighter than usual, as if the water is helping to carry her. Just a few more steps, and she's there.

'Yoho, princess!' the sailor shouts after her. 'Yes, there! Grab it!'

She almost has the chest – but then her foot sinks into a hole. And she goes under!

The good lady Morsegat shrieks, the sailor roars, saltwater fills her nose and her mouth and for a moment she does not know which way is up and which way is down. But then her feet find the bottom, and she pushes herself back up. Seawater streams from her hair and her clothes. Sandy, fishy, salty. She rubs her eyes.

Here she is – and the chest is floating just over there.

'Princess! Come back to shore! At once!'

'I'M COMING,' she splutters. 'I'VE GOT IT!' She pushes the bulky, half-flooded chest ahead of her to the beach. Then she tips it over, until it is lying on its belly in the sand.

The sailor limps closer, fiddles at the lock with his knife, and the lid falls open. Seawater, sand, and a couple of jellyfish who have hitched a ride come pouring out. And a few more things: two soaking-wet shoes, a little wooden box, a board with black and white squares on it, and something black.

The sailor picks up the black thing and wrings it out.

'Bill! You idiot! Look, I've got your hat!' he roars hoarsely across the water. He puts it on his head, and his eyes turn red again.

As punishment, she is sent straight to bed.

'I've never seen you act like that before, princess. Whatever got into you?' The good lady mutters and splutters and follows her with a cloth, wiping water and sand off the floor.

The girl has no answer because she doesn't really know what happened either. She wrings out her stockings and slowly unbuttons her corset.

'Next week Mr Marabou will be coming with the supply boat. He can drop off our guest at a harbour somewhere,' says the good lady Morsegat. 'Then everything can go back to normal, thank goodness.'

'YES, THANK GOODNESS,' says the girl with a nod.

'We still have a lot to do before the big moment.'

'THE BIG…?'

'Before the prince arrives. That happy day. I do hope you haven't forgotten about it?'

'NO,' says the girl. 'OF COURSE I HAVEN'T.'

Prince

The baby princess's aunt stroked the soft spot between her little horns. She had not been invited. The queen still did not wish to receive anyone, not even her sister. But her sister had come anyway.

'I thought it was about time I saw my niece.'

'Well, then take a look,' said the king, pointing. 'Then you can see for yourself.' He had stopped by the door; his sister-in-law was leaning over the huge crib.

'I really don't think it's that bad.'

'Oh, really? Please don't wake it up. She's only just fallen asleep.'

'Yes, absolutely,' said the aunt. 'Those little hairs are so cute.'

'Cute?' The king gave a sour smile. 'It's impossible. Those horns, all that hair, those… A princess can't look like that!'

'Who says so?'

'Everyone says so!' The king's sister-in-law always made him feel a little uncomfortable. She had such terribly piercing eyes. As if she could see straight through him.

'Oh.' The princess's aunt pulled the sheet a little higher over the girl. 'I'm sure you're right. I don't speak to everyone. But well, here she is. What are you going to do about it?'

'We haven't decided yet,' the king said with a sigh. 'We were thinking perhaps of… of…'

'Of simply loving her just as she is?'

'Um…' said the king. 'Well, er, that, um…'

'That's really the only option. You can hardly expect a prince to come sailing along one day and kiss it all better, can you?'

The king sighed again.

'Your sister's having trouble getting used to it.'

'Oh, that sister of mine. She still thinks life is a fairy tale. But we know better, don't we?'

The king shrugged. Was that true? Did he know better?

'What's her name, by the way?'

'Belle.'

'What a beautiful name.'

'Hmm,' said the king gloomily. 'We decided on it before she was born.'

Chess

With Bill's chessboard on his knees, the sailor plays games against the wind, the sea and his drowned companions, but that makes him sadder still, even though he beats them. He misses that bunch, with their smelly feet, big mouths and all. He misses the wind in his face, the swell of the waves beneath his feet. And now here he is, on this strange island with two women, a mean, scrawny one and a big, hairy one with sad eyes. Why are the two of them stuck out here? Doing a bit of schoolwork, out in the middle of the beautiful sea?

That prim woman explained it to him when the girl left the room for a moment, but it is still a mystery to him. Something about a prince on a ship, who will come along one day.

'You don't believe any of that, do you?'

The good lady pursed her lips and looked at the cup in her hand.

'You do not move in those circles. You know nothing about such matters.'

'No, I'm sure you're right,' the sailor mumbled. Thank goodness for that, he thought. He looked around, at the small turret room. How long had the two of them been here? Stacks and stacks of paper everywhere, the shelves bursting with books, embroidery, notebooks filled with the princess's handwriting. The wallpaper mouldy, the curtains frayed, the peeling windows rattling in their frames. And through the windows nothing but an empty stretch of sea.

'She'll be waiting until the cows come home,' he growled. 'Or is that the idea?'

'I am not in a position to question my employer's instructions,' said the good lady Morsegat.

They heard the girl's footsteps in the hallway again. Walking quietly was beyond her.

Here she comes now, walking along the path past his shed. She seems to be walking past more often than she did before, thinks the sailor. On her own, as well. He waves her over.

'Fancy a game? You and me?'

She chuckles shyly.

'**I DON'T KNOW HOW TO PLAY CHESS**,' she says in her thunderous whisper.

'Oh, I can teach you in no time at all.' He puts the board on the chest and arranges the pieces. Black on one side, white on the other. With a bow, he points at the other barrel.

'Please be seated, princess.'

She remains standing, a frown on her face.

'I'm not making fun of you. Go on, playing against you is going to be more fun than playing against people who aren't here, isn't it?'

She stays where she is.

'**I DON'T KNOW IF…**'

'Come on, don't be a spoilsport. Play with me.'

Paw

Her skirt immediately gets sandy and dirty on the barrel. Close up, the sailor is so… She can smell his sweat, sour and wild. *Stormcurse*, she reads on his arm. What does that mean?

He picks up the pieces and names them, one by one. They are black and white and some are wearing little crowns.

'Look, princess. This one's the king. He's what it's all about – got it?'

She nods. Of course, it's always about the king. Her father the king, the father she can barely remember. The prince who will come one day and…

'That king needs to fall.'

'**FALL?**' She looks at him.

'You have to take him down. That's what the game is about. It's called checkmate. Then you win. And this…' He picks up a big black piece with a much smaller crown.

That must be her. Big, dark and ugly. She has to stand in the corner and wait and work and do her best and wait some more.

'Watch how it can jump. Over here and over there. And it can go this way too.' She looks in surprise at the hand holding the black piece. It jumps over horses, towers and bishops. And they fall down.

The sailor goes on talking, shows her how the horses jump, and how the towers move.

'Do you understand, princess?'

She nods and shakes her head a bit, both at the same time.

'Enough talking. Time to play. You start.'

Slowly, she moves a white pawn forward one square.

'Two. Don't be so timid.' He moves his piece. And they're off.

Hesitantly jumping and sliding, they circle each other. Towers straight ahead, bishops diagonally. When she moves the horse the wrong way, he takes her hand.

'No. Like this. Remember?'

She nods and quickly pulls her hand away.

'There we go. You *do* know how to do it. And then I'll do this!' He comes after her with the black bishop. 'Look, this one's got a mean little mouth like the good lady up in the tower. You see?'

She giggles because it's true.

'Go on then, make your move. With your queen!'

She picks up the piece and pauses.

'You know, you could flatten her with one paw,' the sailor says with a grin. 'Easy.'

Paw? It hurts, as if he'd just hit her. She quickly hides her hand in her skirt.

'I HAVE TO GO.'

She pushes back her barrel and stumbles home. He calls something after her, but she doesn't listen.

Up at the tower, the good lady Morsegat is waiting with the tweezers. It's hair removal night. It always hurts, but a princess is supposed to be hairless and smooth. The girl grits her teeth and sits there, gazing out of the window.

The beach is empty, the sailor is probably already curled up on his flour sack. The board with the chess pieces is just as she left it.

Pling plok go the tweezers. Hairs swirl onto the floor.

In the follicles under her skin, another new hair starts to grow every time one is plucked.

Fire

They have not played another game of chess, and suddenly it's Sunday. Tomorrow morning the supply boat will be coming, and it will take the sailor back to shore. The girl's embroidery is sloppier than ever, and she can't seem to grasp the simplest of sums today.

Down on the beach, a fire is burning. The sailor stands in the water, fishing for crabs.

'A farewell meal,' he has told them. 'To say thank you for looking after me.'

He lures the creatures, one by one, using a length of string with some fish on the end. The crabs try to nip him with their pincers, but he just laughs and throws them into the pan, where they angrily hiss.

'Very kind, I'm sure,' mutters the good lady Morsegat, up in the tower. As far as she is concerned, he really needn't have bothered. 'Filth with sand on it, that's all it is. And with far too many calories, princess. You'd have to follow it up with a week of moderation, wouldn't you?'

The girl nods absentmindedly. The classroom smells of festive fish and burning wood. And the good lady Morsegat just seems to be talking for the sake of it.

That night, the lady eats the smallest of bites and perches uncomfortably on her sandy barrel.

'It's getting dark, princess. We need to think about your rest.'

'JUST A LITTLE BIT LONGER?' The girl is sucking on a crab's claw. She had no idea that something that went swimming around the island could be so delicious, so blissfully salty and a little bit sad.

'Rest? Not for ages yet!' The sailor points up at the sky. 'The night is still young. Look at that moon, woman!'

All three of them look up. The moon smiles back at them from the big black sky. The sailor quietly sings the song of the Seven Seas:

> 'The Black Sea isn't black,
> and the Red Sea isn't red.
> The Still Sea isn't still,
> and the Dead Sea's far from dead.

> But the Great Sea, oh, the Great Sea!
> The Great Sea is so wide.
> It's thousands of miles to the other side and…'

'I'm going to bed.' The good lady Morsegat brushes the sand from her dress. 'I expect to see you up at the tower in ten minutes, princess.'

The charred wood glows in the darkness. The sailor throws another branch onto the fire.

'So, what's the story with this prince?' he asks out of nowhere.

Under her hair, the girl flushes a deep red. She is glad that it is dark.

'Is he really coming?'

'OF COURSE HE IS,' she mumbles. 'ONE DAY.'

'And then?'

'THEN, THEN…' What, actually? She has imagined it so many times, at night in her bed. A real prince, who is not scared off by the monster, who will love her just as she is. And then, with a kiss…

Will her monstrous body tear open and will she step out of it as a beautiful princess? Or will it melt away, like wax in a candle flame? Or will it be like magic, with a flash and a bang?

It all seems like such a strange idea, with that living, breathing sailor there beside her. And so unlikely. Just a fairy tale.

In silence, they watch the flames.

'WHAT IS STORMCURSE?' the girl asks after a while.

The sailor's teeth flash in the darkness.

'That is… was our ship. One hell of a tub. Well… Before that blasted storm cursed it to the bottom of the sea.' He sighs. 'But I'll find a new one, when my arm's working again. Plenty of ships out there. Why don't you come with me? Tomorrow?'

'COME WITH YOU?' The very thought of it! What nonsense. What a strange thing to ask.

'The sea is much bigger than this little place, princess. There's room for everything out there. The Still Sea, the Black Sea… The White Cliffs…'

'THE WHITE CLIFFS?' She tastes the name.

'They're far away. So far, far away. But that doesn't matter. All the time in the world.'

She shakes her big head.

'I CAN'T.'

'Why not? All that embroidery. And that prince of yours isn't coming anyway.'

She glares at him.

'OF COURSE HE IS! OF COURSE HE'S COMING… WHEN… ONE DAY. WHEN I'M READY, WHEN…'

'Maybe you'll never be ready,' says the sailor.

She could flatten him with one paw. But she does not do that.

She is a princess.

Waving

At least the little princess's parents came to wave her off. At the crack of dawn, from the jetty at the back of the palace gardens. No one else saw her go.

The trusty Mr Marabou's boat almost took on water when she stepped on board. Her new governess could barely squeeze on to the bench beside her.

The girl looked at the water around the boat. She was a little afraid. All she knew was the inside of the palace.

'WHY CAN'T I…' she began. She had learned to talk but, above all, that she should remain silent. 'WHY CAN'T I JUST STAY HERE?' The sentence had been running through her mind all night long and now she finally dared to say it. She was afraid her father would become angry. And he did.

'We've already spoken about this.'

'BUT IF I… MAYBE… IT'S NOT MY FAULT THAT…'

'Oh, please don't shriek like that!' Her mother pressed a hand to her forehead. Another migraine attack. Maybe she won't have as many headaches, thought the girl. When I'm not here any more.

'No one's saying that it is, girl. Absolutely not. But it's simply what's been decided. We really think it's better this way.'

They waved for a while but stopped before the boat sailed out of sight.

Boat

The trusty Mr Marabou puts sacks and boxes on the shore. He is the good lady Morsegat's brother. The two of them used to be the very best-behaved children in the entire land, she sometimes tells the princess. You can still see that now: they briefly shake hands on arrival and exchange polite nods when he leaves. Anything more would be foolish.

Every second Monday of the month, he brings new supplies and takes away the rubbish. And this time he's taking the sailor too. Carefully, with his good foot, the sailor steps on board.

'You can keep the chessboard,' he has told her. 'Keep practising. For when we see each other again.'

When might that be? the girl thinks. Never, of course.

'See you next month, sister,' says the trusty Mr Marabou with a nod. He is already starting the small engine. The wind is vicious and blows under the skirts of the two women, the big one and the little one.

'Have you thanked the gentleman politely?' asks the little one. 'For everything he's, um, taught us?'

The girl nods and hides her paws behind her back.

'There's no need,' says the sailor. 'And I'd have drowned without you. So, um, cheers for that.'

The girl does not want to look at him but takes a peek anyway. Straight into his big brown eyes. He holds out his good hand to her.

'Are you really not coming?'

'Coming? With us? That monster?' cries the trusty Mr Marabou. 'My poor boat would sink! You'd need a cargo ship for that one, with an iron prow!' He chuckles at his own joke, as he steers away from the jetty. The sound of his laughter can be heard for longer than the engine. But after a while, that, too, disappears and all they can hear is the sea splashing onto the beach.

'Well,' says the good lady Morsegat. 'That was that. Let's get on with today's programme, princess.'

They walk along the path and back to the tower, which is in the middle of the sea. So terribly far from everything.

Virtub

The girl is working on the final letter. With small cross-stitches, she gives it an extra curl. Just one last little flower and she'll be done. And the sampler can join the others in the cupboard.

The good lady Morsegat gives a satisfied nod.

'What shall we do next, princess? I was thinking of ALL'S WELL THAT ENDS WELL myself. How about that?'

She coughs because she caught a cold, last week, by that dirty little fire. The girl has had to walk on her own all week, but she doesn't mind that.

As she goes outside, her head bumps into the top of the door frame. She has grown again. When will she ever stop?

On the beach, his footprints are still everywhere. She can see his studded soles and the deep hole left by his stick. The barrels are beside the burned circle of charcoal, and the chessboard and the pieces are on top of Bill's chest. She has not touched them, and she has not practised. Why would she? She's never going to see him again, anyway. And she doesn't care either.

She is about to walk back along the path, but her feet suddenly head out onto the sand. They follow his footprints, stamping on them and erasing them as she goes.

Good riddance, she thinks. There's no way she's going to miss him. She hopes he's drowned. She'd be glad. She kicks sand over the charcoal and the empty crab claws that are scattered among the remains of the fire.

Away with that rubbish.

She grabs a handful of pieces from the chessboard, walks to the tideline and throws them as far as she can into the sea.

They tumble through the air, making little splashes when they fall. The black king, the queen. The bishop with the mean little mouth follows them. And then all the pawns and horses. The white king.

And that goddamned prince is never coming, of course. *Splash!* – there he goes.

She grabs the board too and sends it sailing through the air. Far from the beach, it comes splashing down and drifts with the wind to the horizon.

Hell's thunder and the pox!

When she looks around, only the black tower remains on the chest. And high up there behind it, the tower she was sent to, a hundred years ago.

'It truly isn't for long,' her father said. 'Just do your best, and the time will fly. Before you know it, the prince will come to fetch you. He really will.'

No one came. Only the sailor, and that was an accident.

Suddenly she really does miss him. And she wants the pieces back. And she wants to sit on a barrel and play his game.

'WAIT!' she shouts. 'GIVE THEM BACK TO ME, SEA!'

She lurches to the tideline, kicks off her shoes and splashes into the waves. She spots the white king at once, and the good lady bishop comes floating by, but she doesn't see the other pieces. She searches and looks and churns up the water, but it is as empty as the beach without the sailor. It stretches all the way to the horizon.

As she walks on, the sea gets higher and higher. The water is cool. Just like before, it makes her lighter. Her feet leave the bottom – and suddenly she is swimming.

She swims, and the more she swims, the less she cares.

When she looks back, everything behind her suddenly seems small, almost insignificant. Even the tall tower. Even though someone up there is shouting, 'Princess, what are you doing? Princess, come back!' The voice blows away on the wind.

Is she really a princess? She doesn't actually know what she is. A girl, a monster, or maybe she's a sea creature, a boat or a fish. Something that can swim on and on without ever getting tired.

She floats on and under the waves, pulling off her dress as she swims, which is completely forbidden, and undoing her corset, which is also most definitely not allowed. Like a big pink jellyfish with buttons, the corset floats away.

She sucks her lungs full of air, and she stretches. The water is so wide. She doesn't bump into anything.

Just a bit longer, she thinks. Just a little way. She really will return to shore soon. Probably still in time for tea.

Seagulls sail above her, and fish swim below. There is enough room for everything.

The Great Sea, oh, the Great Sea, the sailor sings inside her head. *The Great Sea is so wide.*

In the glinting sunlight on the water, it seems as if she sees something. As if, in the distance, a boat is sailing closer. It's just her imagination, of course, but still she sees it: there, and then not there, and then there again.

Here he comes, she thinks. At last. So, today is that happy day. A sail as white as his teeth. Should she wave? Over here, prince!

But she is wet and looks a fright. And she's still far too big and far too hairy. Not to mention half naked. She doesn't wave.

Never mind, she thinks. I don't need to. I don't need a prince any more.

'Yoho, princess!' a voice calls across the water. The boat turns in her direction. It's a cargo boat, she sees, with a sturdy iron prow. Someone leans over the railing and waves.

She sees a flag tied up high on the mast.

As the boat sails closer, she can read the words embroidered on the flag: PATIENCE IS A VIRTUB.

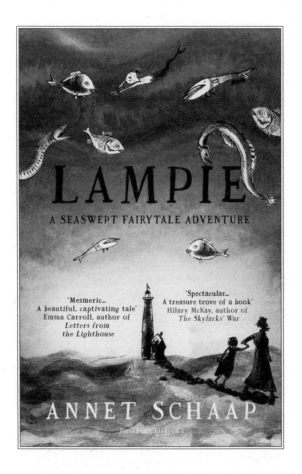

SHORTLISTED FOR THE CARNEGIE MEDAL

'A dark-and-stormy-night of a
fairytale that I absolutely loved'

HILARY MCKAY, *OBSERVER* BEST BOOKS OF THE YEAR

THE TRUE ADVENTURES SERIES

BANDIT'S DAUGHTER
SWORDSWOMAN!
THE BLACK PIMPERNEL
THE FLAG NEVER TOUCHED THE GROUND
THE FOG OF WAR
THE GIRL WHO SAID NO TO THE NAZIS
THE MYSTERIOUS LIFE OF DR BARRY
QUEEN OF FREEDOM

SAVE THE STORY SERIES

THE STORY OF ANTIGONE: ALI SMITH
THE STORY OF GULLIVER: JONATHAN COE
THE STORY OF CAPTAIN NEMO: DAVE EGGERS

THE BLUE DOOR SERIES

THE SWISH OF THE CURTAIN
MADDY ALONE
GOLDEN PAVEMENTS
BLUE DOOR VENTURE
MADDY AGAIN

Pamela Brown

THE WILDWITCH SERIES

WILDFIRE
OBLIVION
LIFE STEALER
BLOODLING

Lene Kaaberbøl

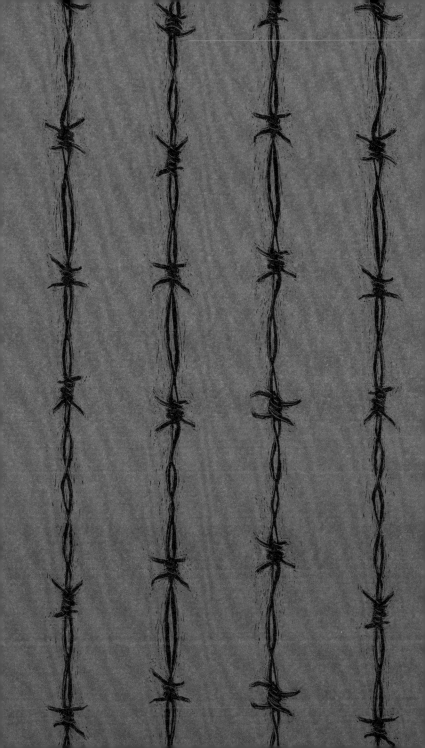